'W

Marco stared at her for a moment, furious that he felt cornered. Damn it, how dared she ask him—accuse him—when *she* was the one who should be called to account? What did it matter why he'd married her when she'd agreed?

Sierra had moved closer to the fire, and the flames cast dancing shadows across her face. She looked utterly delectable wearing his too-big clothes. The belt she'd cinched at her waist showed off its narrowness and the high, proud curve of her breasts. He remembered the feel of them in his hands when he'd given his desire free rein for a few intensely exquisite moments.

That memory had the power to stir the embers of his desire, and he turned away from her, willing the memories and the emotion back. He didn't want to feel anything for Sierra Rocci now. Not even simple lust.

'Damn it, Sierra, you have some nerve, asking me why I behaved the way I did. You're the one who chose to leave without so much as a note.'

'I know.'

'And you still haven't given me a reason why. Don't you th? Your parents abandon, rose. 'S?'

After spending three years as a die-hard New Yorker, **Kate Hewitt** now lives in a small village in the English Lake District with her husband, their five children and a golden retriever. In addition to writing intensely emotional stories, she loves reading, baking and playing chess with her son—she has yet to win against him, but she continues to try. Learn more about Kate at kate-hewitt.com.

Visit the Author Profile page
at millsandboon.co.uk for more titles.

INHERITED
BY FERRANTI

BY
KATE HEWITT

First Published in Great Britain 2016
By Mills & Boon, an imprint of HarperCollins*Publishers*
1 London Bridge Street, London, SE1 9GF

© 2016 Kate Hewitt

ISBN: 978-0-263-91605-8

Printed and bound in Spain
by CPI, Barcelona

INHERITED
BY FERRANTI

CHAPTER ONE

TOMORROW WAS HER wedding day. Sierra Rocci gazed at the fluffy white meringue of a dress hanging from her wardrobe door and tried to suppress the rush of nerves that seethed in her stomach and fluttered up her throat. She was doing the right thing. She had to be. She had no other choice.

Pressing one hand to her jumpy middle, she turned to look out of the window at the darkened gardens of her father's villa on the Via Marinai Alliata in Palermo. The summer night was still and hot, without even a breath of wind to make the leaves of the plane trees in the garden rattle. The stillness felt expectant, even eerie, and she tried to shake off her nervousness; she'd *chosen* this.

Earlier that night she'd dined with her parents and Marco Ferranti, the man she was going to marry. They'd chatted easily, and Marco's gaze had rested on her like a caress, a promise. She could trust this man, she'd told herself. She had to. In less than twenty-four hours she would promise to love, honour and obey him. Her life would be in his hands.

She knew the hard price of obedience. She prayed Marco truly was a gentle man. He'd been kind to her so far, in the three months of their courtship. Gentle and patient, never punishing or pushing, except perhaps for that one time, when they'd gone for a walk in the gardens and he'd kissed her in the shadow of a plane tree, his mouth hard and insistent and surprisingly exciting on hers.

Another leap in her belly, and this was a whole different kind of fear. She was nineteen years old, and she'd only been kissed by her fiancé a handful of times. She was utterly inexperienced when it came to what happened in the bedroom, but Marco had told her, when he'd stopped his shockingly delicious onslaught under the plane tree, that he would be patient and gentle when it came to their wedding night.

She believed him. She'd chosen to believe him—an act of will, a step towards securing her future, her freedom. And yet… Sierra's unfocused gaze rested on the darkened gardens as nerves leapt and writhed inside her and doubt crept into the dark corners of her heart, sly and insidious as that old serpent. Did she really know Marco Ferranti? When she'd first glimpsed him in the courtyard of her father's *palazzo*, she'd watched as one of the kitchen cats had wound its scrawny body around Marco's legs. He'd bent down and stroked the cat's ears and the animal had purred and rubbed against him. Her father would have kicked the cat away, insist its kittens be drowned. Seeing Marco exhibit a moment of unthinking kindness when he thought no one was looking had lit the spark of hope inside Sierra's heart.

She knew her father approved of the marriage between her and Marco; she was not so naïve not to realise that it was his strong hand that had pushed Marco towards her. But she'd encouraged Marco; she'd made a choice. As much as was possible, she'd controlled her own destiny.

On that first evening he'd introduced himself, and then later he had asked her out to dinner. He'd wooed her gently, always courteous, even tender. She wasn't in love with him; she had no interest in that deceitful, dangerous emotion, but she wanted a way out of her father's house and marriage to Marco Ferranti would provide it…if she could truly trust him. She would find out tomorrow, when the vows were said, when the bedroom door closed…

Heaven help her. Sierra bit her knuckles as a fresh wave of fear broke coldly over her. Could she really do this? How could she not? To back out now would be to incur her father's endless wrath. She was marrying in order to be free, and yet she was not free to cry off. Perhaps she would never be truly free. But what other choice was there for a girl like her, nineteen years old and completely cut off from society, from life? Sheltered and trapped.

From below she heard the low rumble of her father's voice. Although she couldn't make out the words, just the sound of his voice had her tensing, alarm prickling the nape of her neck. And then she heard Marco answer, his voice as low as her father's and yet somehow warm. She'd liked his voice the first time she'd heard it, when he'd been introduced to her. She'd liked his smile, too, the quirking of one corner of his mouth, the slow way it lit up his face. She'd trusted him instinctively, even though he worked for her father. Even though he was a man of great power and charm, just as her father was. She'd convinced herself he was different. But what if she'd been wrong?

Before she could lose her nerve Sierra slipped out of her bedroom and hurried halfway down the front stairs, the white marble cold under her bare feet. She paused on the landing, out of view of the men in the foyer below, and strained to listen.

'I am glad to welcome you into my family as a true son.' Her father was at his best, charming and authoritative, a benevolent *papà*, brimming with good will.

'And I am glad to be so welcomed.'

Sierra heard the sound of her father slapping Marco's back and then his good-humoured chuckle. She knew that sound so well. She knew how false it was.

'*Bene*, Marco. As long as you know how to handle Sierra. A woman needs a firm hand to guide her. Don't be too gentle or they get notions. You can't have that.' The words were abhorrent and yet so terribly familiar, the tone gentle, almost amused, her father as assured as ever and completely in control.

Every muscle in Sierra's body seemed to turn to iron as she waited for Marco's response.

'Don't worry, *signor*,' Marco said. 'I know how to handle her.'

Sierra shrank back against the wall, horror and fear churning inside her. *I know how to handle her.* Did he really think that way, like her father did? That she was some beast to be guided and tamed into subservience?

'Of course you do,' Arturo Rocci said, his voice smug with satisfaction. 'I've groomed you myself, chosen you as my son. This is what I wanted, and I could not be more pleased. I have no doubts about you, Marco.'

'You honour me, *signor*.'

'Papà, Marco. You may call me Papà.'

Sierra peeked around the edge of the landing and saw the two men embracing. Then her father gave Marco one more back slap before disappearing down the corridor, towards his study.

Sierra watched Marco, a faint smile curving that mobile mouth, the sharp angle of his jaw darkened with five o'clock shadow, his silvery-grey eyes hooded and sleepy. He'd loosened his tie and shed his suit jacket, and he looked rumpled and tired and overwhelmingly male. *Sexy.*

But there was nothing sexy about what he'd just said. Nothing romantic or loving or remotely attractive about a man who thought women needed to be *handled*. Her stomach clenched hard with fear and, underneath, anger. Anger at Marco Ferranti, for clearly thinking as her father did, and anger at herself for being so naïve to think she actually knew a man after just three months, a handful of arranged dates, all of them carefully orchestrated evenings where Marco was at his best, guiding her gently towards the inevitable conclusion. She'd thought she'd chosen him, but now she wondered how well she'd been manipulated. *Handled*. Perhaps her fiancé was as false as her father, presenting a front she wanted to see while disguising the true man underneath. Would she ever know? Yes, when it was too late. When she was married to him and had no way to escape.

'Sierra?' Marco's silvery gaze flicked upwards, one eyebrow lifted as he gazed at her peeking around the landing, his faint smile deepening, revealing a dimple in one cheek. When Sierra had first seen that dimple it had made him seem friendlier. Kinder. She'd liked him more because of a *dimple*. She felt like such a child, naïve to the point of stupidity, thinking she'd wrested some control for herself when in fact she'd been the merest puppet.

'What are you doing hiding up there?' he asked, and he stretched one hand towards her.

'I…' Sierra licked dry lips as her mind spun. She could not think of a single thing to say. The only thing she could hear on an endless, awful reel was Marco's assured, indulgent words. *I know how to handle her.*

Marco glanced at his watch. 'It's after midnight, so technically I suppose I shouldn't see you. It's our wedding day, after all.'

Wedding day. In just a few hours she would marry this man. She would promise to love him. To honour and obey him…

I know how to handle her.

'Sierra?' Marco asked, concern sharpening his voice. 'Is something wrong?'

Everything was wrong. Everything had been wrong for ever, and she'd actually thought she'd been fixing it. She'd thought she was finally escaping, that she was choosing her own destiny. The thought seemed laughable now. How could she have fooled herself for so long? 'Sierra?' Impatience edged his voice now, and Sierra heard it. Heard how quickly the façade of concern fell away, revealed the true man underneath. Just as it did with her father.

'I'm only tired,' she whispered. Marco beckoned her towards him and on shaking legs she came down the stairs and stood before him, trying not to tremble. Not to show her fear. It was one small act of defiance she'd nurtured for most of her life, because she knew it infuriated her father. He wanted his women to cower and cringe. And Sierra had done her fair share of both, to her shame, over the years. But when she had the strength to stand tall, to act cool and composed, she did. Cloaking herself in numbness had been a way of coping since she was small. She was glad of it now.

Marco cupped her cheek with one hand. His palm was warm and dry and even now the tender gesture sent sparks shooting through her belly, and her legs shook.

'It's not long now,' he murmured, and his thumb brushed her lips. His expression was tender, but Sierra couldn't trust it any more. 'Are you nervous, little one?'

She was terrified. Wordlessly she shook her head. Marco chuckled, the sound indulgent, perhaps patronising. The assumptions she'd made about this man were proving to be just that: assumptions. She didn't really know who he was, what he was capable of. He'd been kind to her, yes, but what if it had just been an act, just like her father's kindness in public was? Marco smiled down at her, his dimple showing. 'Are you certain about that, *mi amore*?'

Mi amore. My love. But Marco Ferranti didn't love her. He'd never said he did, and she didn't even want him to. Looking back, she could see how expedient their relationship had been. A family dinner that led to a walk in the gardens that led to a proper date that led to a proposal. It had been a systematic procedure orchestrated by this man—and her father. And she hadn't realised, not completely. She'd thought she'd had some say in the proceedings, but now she wondered at how well she'd been manipulated. Used.

'I'm all right, Marco.' Her voice came out in a breathy whisper, and it took all the strength she possessed to step away from him so his hand dropped from her cheek. He frowned, and she wondered if he didn't like her taking even that paltry amount of control. She'd let him dictate everything in the three months of their courtship, she realised now. When and where they went, what they talked about—everything had been decided by him. She'd been so desperate to get away, and she'd convinced herself he was a kind man.

'One last kiss,' Marco murmured and before Sierra could think to step farther away he was pulling her towards him, his hands sliding up to cup her face as his lips came down on hers. Hard and soft. Hot and cold. A thousand sensations shivered through her as her lips parted helplessly. Longing and joy. Fear and desire. All of the emotions tangled up together so she couldn't tell them apart. Her hands fisted in his shirt and she stood on her tiptoes to bring his body closer to hers, unable to keep herself from it, not realising how revealing her response was until Marco chuckled and eased her away from him.

'There will be plenty of time later,' he promised her. 'Tomorrow night.'

When they were wed. Sierra pressed her fingers to her lips and Marco smiled, satisfied by her obvious response.

'Goodnight, Sierra,' he said softly, and Sierra managed to choke out a response.

'Goodnight.' She turned and hurried up the stairs, not daring to look back, knowing Marco was watching her.

In the quiet darkness of the upstairs hallway she pressed a hand to her thundering heart. Hated herself, hated Marco, for they were both to blame. She never should have let this happen. She should have never thought she could escape.

Sierra hurried down the hallway to the far wing of the house, knocking softly on the door of her mother's bedroom.

Violet Rocci opened the door a crack, her eyes wide with apprehension. She relaxed visibly when she saw it was Sierra, and opened the door wider to let her daughter in.

'You shouldn't be here.'

'Papà's downstairs.'

'Even so.' Violet clutched the folds of her silk dressing gown together, her face pale with worry and strain. Twenty years ago she'd been a beautiful young woman, a world-class pianist who played in London's best concert halls, on the cusp of major fame. Then she'd married Arturo Rocci and virtually disappeared from the public, losing herself in the process.

'Mamma…' Sierra stared helplessly at her mother. 'I think I may have made a mistake.'

Violet drew her breath in sharply. 'Marco?' Sierra nodded. 'But you love him…' Even after twenty years of living with Arturo Rocci, cringing under his hand, Violet believed in love. She loved her husband desperately, and it had been her destruction.

'I've never loved him, Mamma.'

'What?' Violet shook her head. 'But Sierra, you said…'

'I trusted him. I thought he was gentle. But the only reason I wanted to marry him was to escape…' Even now she couldn't say it. *Escape Papà*. She knew the words would hurt her mother; Violet hid from the truth as much as she could.

'And now?' Violet asked after a moment, her voice low.

'And now I don't know.' Sierra paced the room, the anxiety inside her like a spring that coiled tighter and tighter. 'I realise I don't know him at all.'

'The wedding is tomorrow, Sierra.' Violet turned away from her, her hand trembling at the throat of her dressing gown. 'What can you do? Everything has been arranged—'

'I know.' Sierra closed her eyes as regret rushed through her in a scalding wave. 'I'm afraid I have been very stupid.' She opened her eyes as she blinked back useless tears and set her jaw. 'I know there's nothing I can do. I have to marry him.' Powerlessness was a familiar feeling. Heavy and leaden, a mantle that had weighed her down for far too long. Yet she'd made her own trap this time. In the end she had no one to blame but herself. She'd agreed to Marco's proposal.

'There might be a way.'

Sierra glanced at her mother in surprise; Violet's face was pale, her eyes glittering with uncharacteristic determination. 'Mamma…'

'If you are certain that you cannot go through with it…'

'Certain?' Sierra shook her head. 'I'm not certain of anything. Maybe he is a good man…' *A man who was marrying her for the sake of Rocci Enterprises? A man who worked hand in glove with her father and insisted he knew how to handle her?*

'But,' Violet said, 'you do not love him.'

Sierra thought of Marco's gentle smile, the press of his lips. Then she thought of her mother's desperate love for her father, despite his cruelty and abuse. She didn't love Marco Ferranti. She didn't want to love anyone. 'No, I don't love him.'

'Then you must not marry him, Sierra. God knows a woman can suffer much for the sake of love, but without it…' She pressed her lips together, shaking her head, and questions burned in Sierra's chest, threatened to bubble up her throat. How could her mother love her father, after everything he'd done? After everything she and her mother had both endured? And yet Sierra knew she did.

'What can I do, Mamma?'

Violet drew a ragged breath. 'Escape. Properly. I would have suggested it earlier, but I thought you loved him. I've only wanted your happiness, darling. I hope you can believe that.'

'I do believe it, Mamma.' Her mother was a weak woman, battered into defeated submission by life's hardships and Arturo Rocci's hand. Yet Sierra had never doubted her mother's love for her.

Violet pressed her lips together, gave one quick nod. 'Then you must go, quickly. Tonight.'

'Tonight…?'

'Yes.' Swiftly, her mother went to her bureau and opened a drawer, reached behind the froth of lingerie to an envelope hidden in the back of the drawer. 'It's all I have. I've been saving it over the years, in case…'

'But how?' Numbly, Sierra took the envelope her mother offered her; it was thick with euros.

'Your father gives me housekeeping money every week,' Violet said. Spots of colour had appeared high on each delicate cheekbone, and Sierra felt a stab of pity. She knew her mother was ashamed of how tied she was to her husband, how firmly under his thumb. 'I rarely spend it. And so over the years I've managed to save. Not much…a thousand euros maybe, at most. But enough to get you from here.'

Hope and fear blazed within her, each as strong as the other. 'But where would I go?' She'd never considered such a thing—a proper escape, unencumbered, independent, truly free. The possibility was intoxicating and yet terrifying; she'd spent her childhood in a villa in the country, her adolescent years at a strict convent school. She had no experience of anything, and she knew it.

'Take the ferry to the mainland, and then the train to Rome. From there to England.'

'England…' The land of her mother's birth.

'I have a friend, Mary Bertram,' Violet whispered. 'I have not spoken to her in many years, not since…' Since she'd married Arturo Rocci twenty years ago. Wordlessly, Sierra nodded her understanding. 'She did not want me to marry,' Violet said, her voice so low now Sierra strained to hear it, even when she was standing right next to her mother. 'She didn't trust him. But she told me if anything happened, her door would always be open.'

'You know where she lives?'

'I have her address from twenty years ago. I am afraid that is the best I can do.'

Sierra's insides shook as she considered what she was about to do. She, who did not venture into Palermo without an escort, a guard. Who never handled money, who had never taken so much as a taxi. How could she do this?

How could she not? This was her only chance. Tomorrow she would marry Marco Ferranti, and if he was a man like her father, as his wife she would have no escape. No hope.

'If I leave…' she whispered, her voice thickening. She could not continue, but she didn't need to.

'You will not be able to return,' Violet said flatly. 'Your father would…' She swallowed, shaking her head. 'This will be goodbye.'

'Come with me, Mamma—'

Violet's expression hardened. 'I can't.'

'Because you love him?' The hurt spilled from her like a handful of broken glass, sharp and jagged with pain. 'How can you love him, after everything…?'

'Do not question my choices, Sierra.' Violet's face was pale, her mouth pinched tight. 'But make your own.'

Her own choice. Freedom at last. Overwhelming, frightening freedom, more than she'd ever had before, more than she'd even know what to do with. Instead of shackling herself to a man, even a good man, she would be her own person. Free to choose, to live.

The realisation made her feel sick with fear, dizzy with hope. Sierra closed her eyes. 'I don't know, Mamma…'

'I cannot choose for you, Sierra.' Her mother brushed her cheek lightly with her fingertips. 'Only you can decide your own destiny. But a marriage without love…' Her mother swallowed hard. 'I would not wish that on anyone.'

Not every man is like Arturo Rocci. Not every man is cruel, controlling, hard. Sierra swallowed down the words. Marco Ferranti might not be like her father, but he might very well be. After what she'd heard and realised tonight, she knew she couldn't take the risk.

Her hand clenched on the envelope of euros. Violet nodded, seeing the decision made in Sierra's face. 'God go with you, Sierra.'

Sierra hugged her mother tightly, tears stinging her eyes. 'Quickly now,' Violet said, and Sierra hurried from the room. Down the hall to her own bedroom, the wedding dress hanging from the wardrobe like a ghost. She dressed quickly and then grabbed a bag and stuffed some clothes into it. Her hands shook.

The house was quiet, the night air still and silent. Sierra glanced at the violin case under her bed and hesitated. It would be difficult to bring, and yet…

Music had been her only solace for much of her life. Leaving her violin would be akin to leaving a piece of her soul. She grabbed the case and swung the holdall of clothes over her shoulder. And then she tiptoed downstairs, holding her breath, her heart pounding so hard her chest hurt. The front door was locked for the night, but Sierra slid the bolt from its hinges without so much as a squeak. From the study she heard her father shift in his chair, rustle some papers. For a terrible moment her heart stilled, suspended in her chest as she froze in terror.

Then he let out a sigh and she eased the door open slowly, so slowly, every second seeming to last an hour. She slipped through and closed it carefully behind her before glancing at the dark, empty street. She looked back at the house with its lit windows one last time before hurrying into the night.

CHAPTER TWO

Seven years later

'SHE MIGHT NOT COME.'

Marco Ferranti turned from the window and his indifferent perusal of Palermo's business district with a shrug. 'She might not.' He glanced at the lawyer seated behind the large mahogany desk and then strode from the window, every taut, controlled movement belying the restlessness inside him.

'She didn't come to her mother's funeral,' the lawyer, Roberto di Santis, reminded him cautiously.

Marco's hands curled into fists and he unclenched them deliberately before shoving them into the pockets of his trousers and turning to face the man. 'I know.'

Violet Rocci had died three years ago; cancer had stalked her and killed her in a handful of months. Sierra had not come back for her mother's illness or funeral, despite Arturo's beseeching requests. She had not even sent a letter or card, much to her father's sorrow. The last time Marco had seen her had been the night before their wedding, when he'd kissed her and felt her trembling, passionate response.

The next morning he'd waited at the front of the church of Santa Caterina for his bride to process down the aisle. And waited. And waited. And waited.

Seven years later he was still waiting for Sierra Rocci to show up.

The lawyer shuffled some papers before clearing his throat noisily. He was nervous, impatient, wanting to get the ordeal of Arturo Rocci's will over with. He'd assured Marco it was straightforward if uncomfortable; Marco had seen the document himself, before Arturo had died. He knew what it said. He didn't think Sierra did, though, and he grimly looked forward to acquainting her with its details.

Surely she would come?

Marco had instructed the lawyer to contact her personally. Marco had known where Sierra was for a while; about five years ago, when the first tidal wave of rage had finally receded to a mist, he'd hired a private investigator to discover her whereabouts. He'd never contacted her, never wanted to. But he'd needed to know where she was, what had happened to her. The knowledge that she was living a seemingly quiet, unassuming life in London had not been satisfying in the least. Nothing was.

'She said she would come, didn't she?' he demanded, although he already knew the answer.

When di Santis had called her at her home, she'd agreed to meet here, at the lawyer's office, at ten o'clock on June fifteenth. It was now nearing half past.

'Perhaps we should just begin…?'

'No.' Marco paced the room, back to the window where he gazed out at the snarl of traffic. 'We'll wait.' He wanted to see Sierra's face when the will was read. He wanted to see the expression in her eyes as realisation dawned of how much she'd lost, how much she'd sacrificed simply to get away from him.

'If it pleases you, *signor*,' di Santis murmured and Marco did not bother to answer.

Thirty seconds later the outer door to the building

opened with a telling cautious creak; di Santis's assistant murmured something, and then a knock sounded on the office door.

Every muscle in Marco's body tensed; his nerves felt as if they were scraped raw, every sense on high alert. It had to be her.

'Signor di Santis?' the assistant murmured. 'Signorina Rocci has arrived.'

Marco straightened, forcing himself to relax as Sierra came into the room. She looked exactly the same. The same long, dark blond hair, now pulled back into a sleek chignon, the same wide blue-grey eyes. The same lush mouth, the same tiny, kissable mole at its left corner. The same slender, willowy figure with gentle curves that even now he itched to touch.

Desire flared through him, a single, intense flame that he resolutely quenched.

Her gaze moved to him and then quickly away again, too fast for him to gauge her expression. She stood straight, her shoulders thrown back, her chin tilted at a proud, almost haughty angle. And then Marco realised that she was not the same.

She was seven years older, and he saw it in the faint lines by her eyes and mouth. He saw it in the clothing she wore, a charcoal-grey pencil skirt and a pale pink silk blouse. Sophisticated, elegant clothing for a woman, rather than the girlish dresses she'd worn seven years earlier.

But the inner sense of stillness he'd always admired she still possessed. The sense that no one could touch or affect her. He'd been drawn to that, after the tempest of his own childhood. He'd liked her almost unnatural sense of calm, her cool purpose. Even though she'd only been nineteen she'd seemed older, wiser. *And yet so innocent.*

'Signorina Rocci. I'm so glad you could join us.' Di

Santis moved forward, hands outstretched. Sierra barely brushed her fingertips with his before she moved away, to one of the club chairs. She sat down, her back straight, her ankles crossed, ever the lady. She didn't look at Marco.

He was looking at her, his stare burning. Marco jerked his gaze from Sierra and moved back to the window. Stared blindly out at the traffic that crawled down the Via Libertà.

'Shall we begin?' suggested di Santis, and Marco nodded. Sierra did not speak. 'The will is, in point of fact, quite straightforward.' Di Santis cleared his throat and Marco felt his body tense once more. He knew just how straightforward the will was. 'Signor Rocci, that is, your father, *signorina*—' he gave Sierra an abashed smile that Marco saw from the corner of his eye she did not return '—made his provisions quite clear.' He paused, and Marco knew he was not relishing the task set before him.

Sierra sat with her hands folded in her lap, her chin held high, her gaze direct and yet giving nothing away. Her face looked like a perfect icy mask. 'Could you please tell me what they are, Signor di Santis?' she asked when di Santis seemed disinclined to continue.

The sound of her voice, after seven years' silence, struck Marco like a fist to the gut. Suddenly he was breathless. Low, musical, clear. And yet without the innocent, childish hesitation of seven years ago. She spoke with an assurance she hadn't possessed before, a confidence the years had given her, and somehow this knowledge felt like an insult, a slap in his face. She'd become someone else, someone stronger perhaps, without him.

'Of course, Signorina Rocci.' Di Santis gave another apologetic smile. 'I can go through the particulars, but in essence your father left the bulk of his estate and business to Signor Ferranti.'

Marco swung his gaze to her pale face, waiting for her

reaction. The shock, the regret, the acknowledgement of her own guilt, the realisation of how much she'd chosen to lose. *Something*.

He got nothing.

Sierra merely nodded, her face composed, expressionless. 'The bulk?' she clarified quietly. 'But not all?'

At her question Marco felt a savage stab of rage, a fury he'd thought he'd put behind him years ago. So she was going to be mercenary? After abandoning her family and fiancé, offering no contact for seven long years despite her parents' distress and grief and continued appeals, she still wanted to know how much she'd get.

'No, not all, Signorina Rocci,' di Santis said quietly. He looked embarrassed. 'Your father left you some of your mother's jewellery, some pieces passed down through her family.'

Sierra bowed her head, a strand of dark blond hair falling from her chignon to rest against her cheek. Marco couldn't see her expression, couldn't tell if she was overcome with remorse or rage at being left so little. Trinkets, Arturo had called them. A pearl necklace, a sapphire brooch. Nothing too valuable, but in his generosity Arturo had wanted his daughter to have her mother's things.

Sierra raised her eyes and Marco saw that her eyes glistened with tears. 'Thank you,' she said quietly. 'Do you have them here?'

'I do…' Di Santis fumbled for a velvet pouch on his desk. 'Here they are. Your father left them into my safe-keeping a while ago, when he realised…' He trailed off, and Sierra made no response.

When he realised he was dying, Marco filled in silently. Had the woman no heart at all? She seemed utterly unmoved by the fact that both her parents had died in her absence, both their hearts broken by their daughter's running away. The only thing that had brought her to tears was knowing she'd get nothing more than a handful of baubles.

'They won't be worth much, on the open market,' Marco said. His voice came out loud and terse, each word bitten off. Sierra's gaze moved to him and he felt a deep jolt in his chest at the way she looked at him, her gaze opaque and fathomless. As if she were looking at a complete stranger, and one she was utterly indifferent to.

'Is there anything else I need to know?' Sierra asked. She'd turned back to the lawyer, effectively dismissing Marco.

'I can read the will in its entirety...'

'That won't be necessary.' Her voice was low, soft. 'Thank you for my mother's jewels.' She rose from the chair in one elegantly fluid movement, and Marco realised she was leaving. After seven years of waiting, wondering, wanting a moment where it all finally made sense, he got nothing.

Sierra didn't even look at him as she left the room.

Sierra's breath came out in a shudder as she left the lawyer's office. Her legs trembled and her hands were clenched so tightly around the little velvet pouch that her knuckles ached.

It wasn't until she was out on the street that her breathing started to return to normal, and it took another twenty minutes of driving out of Palermo, navigating the endless snarl of traffic and knowing she'd left Marco Ferranti far behind, before she felt the tension begin to unknot from her shoulders.

The busy city streets gave way to dusty roads that wound up to the hill towns high above Palermo, the Mediterranean glittering blue-green as she drove towards the Nebrodi mountains, and the villa where her mother was buried. When di Santis had rung her, she'd thought about not going to Sicily at all, and then she'd thought about simply going to his office and returning to London on the very same day. She had nothing left in Sicily now.

But then she'd reminded herself that her father couldn't hurt her any longer, that Sicily was a place of ghosts and memories, and not of threats. She'd forgotten about Marco Ferranti.

A trembling laugh escaped her as she shook her head wryly. She hadn't forgotten about Marco; she didn't think she could ever do that. She'd simply underestimated the effect he'd have on her after seven years of thankfully numbing distance.

When she'd first caught sight of him in the office, wearing an expensive silk suit and reeking of power and privilege, looking as devastatingly attractive as he had seven years ago but colder now, so much colder, her whole body had trembled. Fortunately she'd got herself under control before Marco had swung that penetrating iron-grey gaze towards her. She had forced herself not to look at him.

She had no idea how he felt about her seven years on. Hatred or indifference, did it really matter? She'd made the right decision by running away the night before her wedding. She'd never regret it. Watching from afar as Marco Ferranti became more ingrained in Rocci Enterprises, always at her father's side and groomed to be his next-in-line, told her all she needed to know about the man.

The road twisted and turned as it climbed higher into the mountains, the air sharper and colder, scented with pine. The hazy blue sky she'd left in Palermo was now dark with angry-looking clouds, and when Sierra parked the car in front of the villa's locked gates she heard a distant rumble of thunder.

She shivered slightly even though the air was warm; the

wind was picking up, the sirocco that blew from North Africa and promised a storm. The pine trees towered above her, the mountains seeming to crowd her in. She'd spent most of her childhood at this villa, and while she'd loved the beauty and peace of its isolated position high above the nearest hill town, the place held too many hard memories for her to have any real affection for it.

Standing by the window as dread seeped into her stomach when she saw her father's car drive up the winding lane. Fear clenching her stomach hard as she heard his thunderous voice. Cringing as she heard her mother's placating or pleading response. No, she definitely didn't have good memories of here.

But she wouldn't stay long now. She'd see her mother's grave, pay her respects and then return to Palermo, where she'd booked into a budget hotel. By this time tomorrow she'd be back in London, and she'd never come to Sicily again.

Quickly, Sierra walked along the high stone wall that surrounded the estate. She knew the property like her own hand; she and her mother had always stayed here until Arturo called them into service, to play-act at being the perfect family for various engagements or openings of the Rocci hotels that now graced much of the globe. Her mother had lived for her husband's summons; Sierra had dreaded them.

Away from the road she knew the wall had crumbled in places, creating a gap low enough for her to climb over. She doubted her father had seen to repairs in the last seven years; she wondered if he'd come to the villa at all. He'd preferred to live his own life in Palermo except when he needed his wife and daughter to play at happy families for the media.

She stepped into the shelter of a dense thicket of pine

trees, the world falling to darkness as the trees overhead shut out any remnant of sunlight. Thunder rumbled again, and the branches snagged on her silk blouse and narrow skirt, neither a good choice for walking through woods or climbing walls.

After a few moments of walking she came to a crumbled section of wall and with effort, thanks to her pencil skirt, she managed to clamber over it. Sierra let out a breath of relief and started towards the far corner of the estate, where the family cemetery was located.

She skirted the villa, not wanting to attract attention to herself; she had no idea if anyone was in residence. Arturo had installed a housekeeper when she'd lived here with her mother, a beady-eyed old woman who had been her father's henchman and spy. If she was still here, Sierra had no wish to attract her attention.

In the distance the ghostly white marble headstones of the Rocci family plot appeared through the stormy gloom like silent, still ghosts, and Sierra's breath caught in her throat as she approached. She knew where her mother's marker lay, in the far corner; it was the only one that hadn't been there when she'd left.

Violet Rocci, Beloved Wife

She stared at the four words written starkly on the tombstone until they blurred and she blinked back tears. Beloved mother, yes, but *wife*? Had her father loved her mother at all? Sierra knew Violet believed so, but Sierra wanted to believe love was better and bigger than that. Love didn't hurt, didn't punish or belittle. She wanted to believe that, but she didn't know if she could. She certainly had no intention of taking the risk of finding out for herself.

'*Ti amo*, Mamma,' she whispered, and rested her hand on top of the cool marble. She'd missed her mother so much over these past seven years. Although she'd written Violet a few letters over the years, her mother had discouraged contact, fearing for Sierra's safety. The few letters she'd had were precious and all too rare, and had stopped completely well before Violet's illness.

She drew a deep breath and willed the tears away. She wouldn't cry now. There had been enough sadness already. Another deep breath and her composure was restored, as she needed it to be. Cloak herself in coolness, keep the feelings at bay. She turned away from the little cemetery plot and started walking back towards her car. She hoped Violet Rocci was at peace now, safe from her husband's cruelty. It was the smallest comfort, but the only one she could cling to now.

Thunder rumbled and forked lightning split the sky as the first heavy raindrops fell. Sierra ducked her head and started hurrying back to the section of wall she'd climbed over. She didn't want to be caught in a downpour, and neither did she relish the drive back down the steep mountain roads in this weather.

She climbed over the wall and hurried through the stand of pines, the branches snagging on her blouse and hair as the rain fell steadily, soaking her. Within seconds her pink silk blouse was plastered to her skin and her hair fell out of its chignon in wet rat's tails.

She cursed under her breath, thankful to emerge from the trees, only to have her insides freeze as she caught sight of a second car, a dark SUV, parked behind her own. As she came onto the road the door to the car opened, and an all too familiar figure emerged.

Marco Ferranti strode towards her, his white dress shirt soon soaked under the downpour so every well-defined muscle was outlined in glorious detail. Sierra flicked her gaze upwards, but the anger she saw snapping in his eyes, the hard set of his mouth and jaw, made her insides quell and she looked away. The rain was sheeting down now and she stopped a few feet from him, sluicing rainwater from her face.

'So.' Marco's voice was hard, without a shred of warmth. 'What the bloody hell do you think you're doing here?'

CHAPTER THREE

SIERRA DREW A deep breath and pushed the sodden mass of her hair away from her face. 'I was paying my respects.' She tried to move past him to her car but he blocked her way. 'What are *you* doing here?' she challenged, even though inside she felt weak and shaky with fear. Here was the real man Marco had hidden from her before, the angry, menacing man who loomed above her like a dark shadow, fierce and threatening. But, just as with her father, she wouldn't show her fear to this man.

'It's my home,' Marco informed her. 'As of today.'

She recoiled at that, at the triumph she heard in his tone. He was glad he'd got it all, and that she'd got almost nothing. Of course he was. 'I hope you enjoy it then,' she bit out, and his mouth curved in an unpleasant smile.

'I'm sure I will. But you were trespassing on private property, you do realise?'

She shook her head, stunned by the depth of his anger and cruelty. So this was the true face of the man she'd once thought of marrying. 'I'm leaving anyway.'

'Not so fast.' He grabbed her arm, his powerful fingers encircling her wrist, making her go utterly still. The commanding touch was so familiar and instinctively she braced herself for a blow. But it didn't come; Marco simply stared at her, and it took Sierra a moment to realise the fingers around her wrist were actually exerting only a gentle pressure.

'I want to know why you were here.'

'I told you,' she bit out. 'To pay my respects.'

'Did you go inside the villa?'

She stared at him, nonplussed. 'No.'

'How do I know that? You might have stolen something.'

She let out an incredulous laugh. If she'd had any doubts about whether jilting Marco Ferranti had been the right thing to do, he was dispelling them with dizzying speed.

'What on earth do you think I stole?' She shook his hand off her wrist and spread her arms wide. 'Where would I hide it?' She saw Marco's gaze flick down to her breasts and too late she realised the white lace bra she wore was visible through the soaked, near-transparent silk. Sierra kept her head held high with effort.

'I can't be sure of anything when it comes to you, except that you can't be trusted.'

'Did you follow me all the way from Palermo?'

His jaw tightened. 'I wanted to know where you were going.'

'Well, now you know. And now I'm going back to Palermo.' She started to move away but Marco stilled her with one outflung hand. He nodded towards the steep, curving road that led down the mountain.

'The road will be impassable now with flash flooding. You might as well come into the villa until it is over.'

'And you'll frisk me for any possible stolen goods?' Sierra finished. 'I'll take my chances with the flooding.'

'Don't be stupid.' Marco's voice was harsh, dismissive, reminding her so much of her father. Clearly, he'd decided to emulate his mentor.

'I'm not being stupid,' she snapped. 'I mean every word I say.'

'You'd rather risk serious injury or even death than come into a dry house with me?' Marco's mouth twisted. 'What did I ever do to deserve such disgust?'

'You just accused me of *stealing*.'

'I simply wanted to know why you were here.'

Above them an ear-splitting crack of thunder sounded, making Sierra jump. She was completely soaked and unfortunately she knew Marco spoke the truth. The roads would be truly impassable, most likely for some time.

'Fine,' she said ungraciously and got into her car.

Marco unlocked the gates with the remote control in his car, and they swung silently back, revealing the villa's long, curving drive.

Taking a deep breath, Sierra drove up with Marco following like her jailer. As soon as his car had passed, the gates swung closed again, locking her inside.

She parked in front of the villa and turned off the engine, reluctant to get out and face Marco again. And to face all the unwelcome memories that crowded her brain and heart. Coming back to Sicily had been a very bad idea.

Her door jerked open and Marco stood there, glowering at her. 'Are you going to get out of your car?'

'Yes, of course.' She climbed out, conscious of his nearness, of the animosity rolling off him even though he'd sounded cold and controlled. After seven years, did he still hate her for what she'd done? It seemed so.

'Is anyone living in the villa?' she asked as he pressed the security code into the keypad by the front door.

'No. I've left it empty for the time being, while I've been in Palermo.' He glanced back at her, his expression opaque. 'While your father was in hospital.'

Sierra made no reply. The lawyer, di Santis, had told her

that her father had died of pancreatic cancer. He'd had it for several years but had kept it secret; when the end came it had been swift. After the call she'd tried to dredge up some grief for the man who had sired her; she'd felt nothing but a weary relief that he was finally gone.

Marco opened the front door and ushered her into the huge marble foyer. The air was chilly and stale, the furniture shrouded in dust cloths. Sierra shivered.

'I'll turn the hot water on,' Marco said. 'I believe there are clothes upstairs.'

'My clothes…?'

'No, those were removed some time ago.' His voice was clipped, giving nothing away. 'But some of my clothes are in one of the guest bedrooms. You can borrow something to wear while your own clothes dry.'

She remained shivering in the foyer, dripping rainwater onto the black and white marble tiles, while Marco set about turning on lights and removing dust covers. It felt surreal to be back in this villa, and she couldn't escape the clawing feeling of being trapped, not just by the locked gates and the memories that mocked her, but by the man inhabiting this space, seeming to take up all the air. She felt desperate to leave.

'I'll light a fire in the sitting room,' Marco said. 'I'm afraid there isn't much food.'

'I don't need to eat. I'm going to leave as soon as possible.'

Marco's mouth twisted mockingly as he glanced back at her. 'Oh, I don't think so. The roads will be flooded for a while. I don't think you'll be leaving before tomorrow morning.' His eyes glinted with challenge or perhaps derision as he folded his powerful arms across his chest. Even angry and hostile, he was a beautiful man, every taut muscle radiating strength and power. But she didn't like brute strength. She hated the abuse of power. She looked away from him.

'Why don't you take a bath and change?'

Sierra's stomach clenched at the prospect of spending a night under the same roof as Marco Ferranti. Of taking a bath, changing clothes…everything making her feel vulnerable. He must have seen something in her face for he added silkily, 'Surely you're not worried for your virtue? Trust me, *cara*, I wouldn't touch you with a ten-foot bargepole.'

She flinched at both the deliberate use of the endearment and the contempt she saw in his face. The casual cruelty had been second nature to her father, but it stung coming from Marco Ferranti. He'd been kind to her once.

'Good,' she answered when she trusted her voice. 'Because that's the last thing I'd want.'

His gaze darkened and he took a step towards her. 'Are you sure about that?'

Sierra held her ground. She knew her body had once responded to Marco's, and even with him emanating raw, unadulterated anger she had a terrible feeling it would again. A single caress or kiss and she might start to melt, much to her shame. 'Very sure,' she answered in a clipped voice, and then she turned towards the stairs without another word.

She found Marco's things in one of the guest bedrooms; he hadn't taken the master bedroom for himself and she wondered why. It was all his now, every bit of it. The villa, the *palazzo* in Palermo, the Rocci business empire of hotels and real estate holdings. Her father had given everything to the man he'd seen as a son, and left his daughter with nothing.

Or almost nothing. Carefully she took the velvet pouch out from the pocket of her skirt. The pearl necklace and sapphire brooch that had been her mother's before she mar-

ried were hers now. She had no idea why her father had al-
lowed her to have them; had it been a moment of kindness
on his deathbed, or had he simply been saving face, trying to seem like the kind, grieving father he'd never been?

It didn't matter. She had a keepsake to remind her of
her mother, and that was all she'd wanted.

Quickly, Sierra slipped out of her wet clothes and took
a short, scaldingly hot shower. She dressed in a soft grey
T-shirt and tracksuit bottoms of Marco's; it felt bizarrely
intimate to wear his clothes, and they swam on her. She
used one of his belts to keep the bottoms from sliding right
off her hips, and combed her hair with her fingers, leaving it hanging damply down her back.

Then, hesitantly, she went downstairs. She would have
rather hidden upstairs away from Marco until the storm
passed but, knowing him, he'd most likely come and find
her. Perhaps it would be better to deal with the past, get
that initial awful conversation out of the way, and then they
could declare a silent truce and ignore each other until she
was able to leave.

She found him in the sitting room, crouched in front of
the fire he was fanning into crackling flame. He'd changed
into jeans and a black T-shirt and the clothes fitted him
snugly, emphasising his powerful chest and long legs,
every inch of him radiating sexual power and virility.

Sierra stood in the doorway, conscious of a thousand
things: how Marco's damp hair had started to curl at the
nape of his neck, how the soft cotton of the T-shirt she
wore—*his* T-shirt—rubbed against her bare breasts. She
felt a tingling flare of what could only be desire and tried to
squelch it. He hated her now, and in any case she knew what
kind of man he was. How could she possibly desire him?

He glanced back at her as she came into the room, and
with a shivery thrill she saw an answering flare of aware-

ness in his own eyes. He straightened, the denim of his jeans stretching across his powerful thighs, and Sierra's gaze was drawn to the movement, to the long, fluid length of his legs, the powerful breadth of his shoulders. Once he would have been hers, a thought that had filled her with apprehension and even fear. Now she felt a flicker of curiosity and even loss for what might have been, and she quickly brushed it aside.

The man was handsome. Sexy. She'd always known that. It didn't change who he was, or why she'd had to leave.

'Come and get warm.' Marco's voice was low, husky. He gestured her forward and Sierra came slowly, reluctant to get any closer to him. Shadows danced across the stone hearth and her bare feet sank into the thick, luxuriously piled carpet.

'Thank you,' she murmured without looking at him. The tension in the room was thick and palpable, a thousand unspoken words and thoughts between them. Sierra stared at the dancing flames, having no idea how to break the silence, or whether she wanted to. Perhaps it would be better to act as if the past had never happened.

'When do you return to London?' Marco asked. His voice was cool, polite, the question that of an acquaintance or stranger.

Sierra released the breath she'd bottled in her lungs without realising. Maybe he would make this easy for her. 'Tomorrow.'

'Did you not think you'd have affairs to manage here?'

She glanced at him, startled, saw how his silvery eyes had narrowed to iron slits, his mouth twisted mockingly. His questions sounded innocuous, but she could see and feel the latent anger underneath the thin veneer of politeness.

'No. I didn't expect my father to leave me anything in his will.'

'You didn't?' Now he sounded nonplussed, and Sierra shrugged.

'Why would he? We've neither spoken nor seen each other in seven years.'

'That was your choice.'

'Yes.'

They were both silent, the only sound the crackling of the fire, the settling of logs in the grate. Sierra had wondered how much Marco guessed of her father's abuse and cruelty. How much he would have sanctioned. The odd slap? The heaping of insults and emotional abuse? Did it even matter?

She'd realised, that night she'd left, that she could not risk it. She'd been foolish to think she could, that she could entrust herself to any man. Leaving Marco had been as much about her as about him.

'Why did you come back here, to this villa?' Marco asked abruptly, and Sierra looked up from her contemplation of the fire.

'I told you—'

'To pay your respects. To what? To whom?'

'To my mother. Her grave is in the family plot on the estate.'

He cocked his head, his silvery gaze sweeping coldly over her. 'And yet you didn't return when your mother was ill. You didn't even send a letter.'

Because she hadn't known. But would she have come back, even if she had known? Could she have risked her father's wrath, being under his hand once more? Sierra swallowed and looked away.

'No answer?' Marco jibed softly.

'You know the answer. And anyway, it wasn't a question.'

He shook his head slowly. 'You are certainly living up—or should I say down—to my expectations.'

'What does that mean?'

'For seven years I've wondered just how cold a bitch I almost married. Now I know.'

The words felt like a slap, sending her reeling. She blinked past the pain, told herself it didn't matter. 'You can think what you like.'

'Of course I can. It's not as if you've ever given me any answers, have you? Any possible justification for what you did, not just in leaving me, but in deserting your family?'

She didn't reply. She didn't want to argue with Marco, and in any case he hadn't really been asking her a question. He'd been stating a fact, making a judgement. He'd made his mind up about her years ago, and nothing she could say would change it now, not even the truth. Besides, he'd been her father's right-hand man for over a decade. Either he knew how her father had treated his family, or he'd chosen not to know.

'You have nothing to say, Sierra?'

It was the first time he'd called her by her first name and it sent a shiver of apprehensive awareness rippling through her. He sounded so *cold*. For one brief blazing second she remembered the feel of his lips on hers when he'd kissed her in the garden. His hands on her body, sliding so knowingly up to cup her breasts; the electric tingle of excitement low in her belly, kindling a spark she hadn't even known existed, because no man had ever touched her that way. No man had ever made her feel so desired.

Mentally, Sierra shrugged away the memory. So the man could kiss. Marco Ferranti no doubt had unimaginable sexual prowess. He'd probably been with dozens—hundreds—of women. It didn't change facts.

'No,' she told him flatly. 'I have nothing to say.'

* * *

Marco stared at Sierra, at the cool hauteur on her lovely face, and felt another blaze of anger go off like a firework in his gut. How could she be so cold?

'You know, I admired how cool you were, all those years ago,' he told her. Thankfully, his voice sounded as flat as hers, almost disinterested. He'd given away too much already, too much anger, too much emotion. He'd had seven years to get over Sierra. In any case, it wasn't as if he'd ever loved her.

'Cool?' Sierra repeated. She looked startled, wary.

'Yes, you were so self-possessed, so calm. I liked that about you.' She didn't reply, just watched him guardedly. 'I didn't realise,' Marco continued, his tone clipped as he bit off each word precisely, 'that it was because you had no heart. You were all ice underneath.' Except she hadn't been ice in his arms.

Still she said nothing, and Marco could feel the anger boiling inside him, threatening to spill out. 'Damn it, Sierra, didn't you ever think that I deserved an explanation?'

Her gaze flicked away from his and her tongue darted out to touch her lips. Just that tiny gesture set lust ricocheting through him. He felt dizzy from the excess of emotion, anger and desire twined together. He didn't want to feel so much. After seven years of cutting himself off from such feelings, the force of their return was overwhelming and unwelcome.

'Well?' Marco demanded. Now that he'd asked the question, he realised he wanted an answer.

'I thought it was explanation enough that I left,' Sierra said coolly.

Marco stared at her, his jaw dropping before he had the presence of mind to snap it shut, the bones aching. 'How on earth could you think that?'

Her gaze moved to his and then away again. 'Because it was obvious I'd changed my mind.'

'Yes, I do realise. But I've never understood why, and your father didn't, either. He was devastated when you left, you know. Utterly bereft.' He still remembered how Arturo had wept and embraced him when he'd told him, outside the church, that Sierra was gone. Marco had been numb, disbelieving; he'd wanted to send search parties until the truth of what Arturo was saying slammed home. She wasn't missing. She'd *left*. She'd left him, and for a second he wasn't even surprised. His marriage to Sierra, his acceptance into the Rocci family, it had all been too good—too wonderful—to be true.

Now Sierra's mouth firmed and she folded her arms, her blue-grey eyes turning as cold as the Atlantic on a winter's day. 'Why did you want to marry me, Marco, if we're going to rake through the past? I never quite understood that.' She paused, her cool gaze trained on him now, unflinching and direct, offering an unspoken challenge. 'It's not because you loved me.'

'No.' He could admit that much. He hadn't known her well enough to love her, and in any case he'd never been interested in love. Love meant opening yourself up to emotional risk, spreading your arms wide and inviting someone to take a shot. In his mother's case, she'd sustained a direct hit. Not something he'd ever be so foolish or desperate to do.

'So?' Sierra arched an eyebrow, and it disconcerted him how quickly and neatly she'd flipped the conversation. He was no longer the one on the attack. How dare she put him on the defensive—she, who'd walked away without a word?

'I could ask the same of you,' he said. 'Why did you agree to marry me?' *And then change your mind?*

Sierra's mouth firmed. 'I'd convinced myself I could be happy with you. I was wrong.'

'And what made you decide that?' Marco demanded.

She sighed, shrugging her slim shoulders. 'Do we really want to go through all this?' she asked. 'Do you think it will help? So much has happened. Seven years, Marco. Maybe we should just agree to—'

'Disagree? We're not talking about a little spat we had, Sierra. Some petty argument.' His voice came out harshly—too harsh, ragged and revealing with the force of his emotion. Even so, he couldn't keep himself from continuing. 'We're talking about *marriage*. We were a few hours away from pledging our lives to one another.'

'I know.' Her lips formed the words but he could barely hear her whisper. Her face had gone pale, her eyes huge and dark. Still she stood tall, chin held high. She had strength—more strength than he'd ever realised—but right now it only made him angry.

'Then why…?'

'You still didn't answer my question, Marco.' Her chin tilted up another notch. 'Why did you want to marry me?'

He stared at her for a moment, furious that he felt cornered. 'I need a drink,' he said abruptly, and stalked into the kitchen. She didn't follow him.

He yanked a bottle of whisky from the cupboard and poured a healthy measure that he downed in one swallow. Then he poured another.

Damn it, how dare she ask him, accuse *him*, when she was the one who should be called to account? What did it matter why he'd wanted to marry her, when she'd agreed?

He drained his second glass and then went back to the sitting room. Sierra had moved closer to the fire and the flames cast dancing shadows across her face. Her hair was starting to dry, the ends curling. She looked utterly delectable wearing his too-big clothes. The T-shirt had slipped off one shoulder, so he could see how golden and smooth her skin was. The belt she'd cinched at her waist showed off its narrowness and the high, proud curve of her breasts. He remembered the feel of them in his hands, when he'd given his desire free rein for a few intensely exquisite moments. He'd felt her arch into him, heard her breathy gasp of pleasure.

The memory now had the power to stir the embers of his desire and he turned away from her, willing the memories, the emotion, back. He didn't want to feel anything, not even simple lust, for Sierra Rocci now.

'Damn it, Sierra, you have some nerve asking me why I behaved the way I did. You're the one who chose to leave without so much as a note.'

'I know.'

'And you still haven't given me a reason why. You changed your mind. Fine. I accept that. It was patently obvious at the time.' His voice came out sharp with bitterness and he strove to moderate it. 'But you still haven't said why. Don't you think I deserve an explanation? Your parents are no longer alive to hear why you abandoned them, but I am.' His voice hardened, rose. 'So why don't you just tell me the truth?'

CHAPTER FOUR

A LOG SETTLED in the grate and popped, sparks scattering across the hearth before turning to cold ash. The silence stretched on and Sierra let it. What could she say? What would Marco believe or be willing to hear?

It was obvious he'd manufactured his own version of events, no doubt been fed lies by her father, who would have pretended to grieve for her. Marco wouldn't believe the truth now, even if she fed it to him with a spoon.

'Well?' His voice rang out, harsh and demanding. 'No reply?'

She shrugged, not meeting his gaze. 'What do you want me to say?'

'I told you—the truth. Why did you leave, Sierra? The night before our wedding?'

Sierra took a deep breath and forced herself to meet his hard gaze; looking into his eyes felt like slamming into a wall. 'Fine. The truth is I had second thoughts. Cold feet. I realised I was putting my life in the hands of a virtual stranger, and that it was a mistake. I couldn't do it.'

He stared at her, his gaze like concrete, a muscle flickering in his jaw. 'You realised all this the night before our wedding? It didn't occur to you at any point during the month of our engagement?'

'I'd thought I was making the right decision. That night I realised I wasn't.'

He shook his head derisively. 'You make it sound so simple.'

'In some ways it was, Marco.' Another deep breath. 'We didn't love or even know each other, not really. We'd had a handful of dates, everything stage-managed by my father. Our marriage would have been a disaster.'

'You can be so sure?'

'Yes.' She looked away, wanting to hide the truth she feared would be reflected in her eyes. She *wasn't* sure. Not completely. Maybe their marriage would have worked. Maybe Marco really was a good and gentle man. Although the fact that he'd remained at her father's right hand since then made her wonder. Doubt. How much of her father's shallow charm and ruthless ways had rubbed off on her ex-fiancé? Judging from the cold anger she'd seen from him today, she feared far too much. No, she'd made the right choice. She had to believe that.

'Fine.' Marco exhaled in one long, low rush of breath. 'You changed your mind. Why didn't you tell me, then? Talk to me and tell me what you were thinking? Did I not deserve that much courtesy? A note, at the very least? Maybe I could have convinced you…'

'Exactly. You would have convinced me.' He stared at her, nonplussed, and she continued, 'I was nineteen, Marco. You were a man of nearly thirty, sophisticated and worldly, especially compared to me. I had no life experience at all, and I was afraid to stand up to you, afraid that you'd sweep my arguments aside and then I'd marry you out of fear.'

'Did I ever give you any reason to be afraid of me?' he demanded. 'What a thing to accuse me of, Sierra, and with

no proof.' His voice vibrated with anger and she fought
not to flinch.

Now was the time to say it. To admit what she'd overheard, how it had made her feel. Why shouldn't she? What
did she have to lose? She'd lost it all already. She'd gained
a new life—a small, quiet life that was safe and was *hers*.
She had nothing she either needed or wanted from this
man. 'I heard you,' she said quietly.

His gaze widened and his mouth parted soundlessly
before he finally spoke. 'You *heard* me? Am I supposed
to know what that means?'

'The night before our wedding, I heard you talking to
my father.'

He shook his head slowly, not understanding. Not wanting to understand. 'I'm still in the dark, Sierra.'

A deep breath, and she let it buoy her lungs, her courage. 'You said, "I know how to handle her", Marco.' Even
after all the years the memory burned. 'When my father
told you how women get notions. You spoke about me as
if I were a dog, a beast to be bridled. Someone to be managed rather than respected.'

A full minute passed where Marco simply stared at her.
Sierra held his gaze even though she ached to look away.
To hide. The fire crackled and a spark popped, the loud
sound breaking the stillness and finally allowing her to
look somewhere else.

'And for this, this one statement I can't even remember,'
Marco said in a low voice, 'you condemned me? Damned
me?'

'It was enough.'

He swore, a hiss under his breath. Sierra flinched, tried
not to cringe. A man's anger still had the power to strike
fear into her soul. Make her body tense as she waited to
ward off the blow.

'How could you—' He broke off, shaking his head. 'I don't even want to know. I'm not interested in your excuses.' He stalked into the kitchen. After a moment Sierra followed him. She'd rather creep back upstairs but she felt the conversation needed to be finished. Maybe then the past would be laid to rest, or at least as much as it could be.

She stood in the doorway while he opened various cupboards, every movement taut with suppressed fury.

He took out a packet of dried pasta and tossed it onto the granite island. 'I'm afraid there's not much to eat.'

'I'm not hungry.'

'Don't be perverse. You probably haven't eaten anything all day. You should keep up your strength.'

The fact that he was right made Sierra stay silent. She was being perverse because she didn't want to spend any more time with him than necessary. Her stomach growled loudly and Marco gave her a mocking look.

Sierra forced a smile. 'Very well, then. Let me help.' He shrugged his indifferent assent and Sierra moved awkwardly through the kitchen, conscious how this cosy domestic scene was at odds with the tension and animosity that still tautened the air.

They worked in silence for a few minutes, concentrating on mundane things; Sierra found a large pot and filled it with water, plonking it on the huge state-of-the-art range as Marco retrieved a tin of crushed tomatoes and various herbs from the cupboards.

This was his home now, and yet it once had been hers. She glanced round the huge kitchen, the oak table in the dining nook where she'd eaten breakfast while her mother moped and drank espresso. Sierra had enjoyed a cautious happiness at the villa, but Violet had always been miserable away from Arturo.

Sierra shook her head at the memory, at the regret she still felt for her mother's life, her mother's choices.

Marco noticed the movement and stilled. 'What is it?'

She turned to him. 'What do you mean?'

'You're shaking your head. What are you thinking about?'

'Nothing.'

'Something, Sierra.'

'I was just thinking about my mother. How I missed her.'

His eyebrows rose in obvious disbelief. 'Why didn't you ever come back, then?'

The question hung in the air, taunting her. She could tell him the truth, but she resisted instinctively. Sierra didn't know if it was because she didn't want to be pitied, or because she suspected he wouldn't believe her. Or, worse, an innate loyalty to her father, a man who had shown her so much contempt and disgust.

She drew a deep breath. 'I couldn't.'

'Why not?'

'My father would not want me back, after…everything.'

'You're wrong.' She recoiled at the flatly spoken statement. He could be so sure? 'You judge people so quickly, Sierra. Me and your father both. He would have welcomed you back with open arms, I know it. He told me as much, many times.'

She leaned against the counter, absorbing his statement. So her father had been feeding him lies all along, just as she'd suspected. She could tell Marco believed what he said, deeply and utterly. And he would never believe her.

'I suppose I wasn't prepared to risk it.'

'You broke his heart,' Marco told her flatly. 'And your mother's. Neither of them were ever the same.'

Guilt curdled her stomach like sour milk. She'd always

known, even if she hadn't wanted to dwell on it, that her leaving would cost her mother. It hurt to hear it now. 'How do you know? Did you see my mother very much?'

'Often enough. Arturo invited me to dinner many times. Your mother became reclusive—'

'She was always reclusive,' Sierra cut in sharply. She could not let every statement pass as gospel. 'We lived here, at the villa, except when my father called us into action.'

'A country life is better for children.' He glanced round the huge kitchen, spreading one arm wide to encompass the luxurious villa and its endless gardens. 'This would be a wonderful place to raise children.' His voice had thickened, and with a jolt Sierra wondered if he was thinking about their children. The thought made her feel a strangely piquant sense of loss that she could not bear to consider too closely.

'So how was she more reclusive?'

'She didn't always join us for meals. She didn't come to as many social events. Her health began to fail…'

Tears stung Sierra's eyes and she blinked rapidly to dispel them. She didn't want Marco to see her cry. She could guess why her mother had retreated more. Her father must have been so angry with her leaving, and he would have taken it out on her mother. She'd have had no choice but to hide.

'The truth hurts, does it?' Marco said, his voice close to a sneer. He'd seen her tears and he wasn't impressed. 'I suppose it was easy to forget about them from afar.'

'None of it was easy,' Sierra choked out. She drew a deep breath and willed the grief back. Showing Marco how much she was affected would only make him more contemptuous. He'd judged her long ago and nothing she could do or say would change the way he felt about her.

And it shouldn't matter, because after today she would never see him again.

A prospect that caused her an absurd flash of pain; she forced herself to shrug it off.

'It seemed easy from where I stood,' Marco answered. His voice was sharp with bitterness.

'Maybe it did,' Sierra agreed. 'But what good can it do now, to go over these things? What do you want from me, Marco?'

What did he want from her? Why was he pushing her, demanding answers she obviously couldn't or didn't want to give? Did it even matter which? It was seven years ago. She'd had cold feet, changed her mind, whatever. She'd treated both him and her parents callously, and he was glad to have escaped a lifetime sentence with a woman as cold as she was. They'd both moved on.

Except when he'd seen her standing in the doorway of di Santis's office, when he'd remembered how she'd tasted and felt and even more, how he'd enjoyed being with her, seeing her shy smile, the way those blue-grey eyes had warmed with surprised laughter...when he'd been looking forward to the life they would build together... It didn't feel as if he'd moved on. At all. And that realisation infuriated him.

Marco swung away from her, bracing his hands against the counter. 'I don't want anything from you. Not any more.' He busied himself with opening the tin of tomatoes and pouring the contents into a pan. 'Seeing you again has made me ask some questions,' he answered, his voice thankfully cool. 'And want some answers. Since I never had any.'

'I can understand that.' She sounded sad.

'Can you?' *Then why...?* But he wouldn't ask her anything more. He wouldn't beg. Wordlessly, he turned back to their makeshift meal. Sierra watched him, saying nothing, but Marco felt the tension ease slightly. The anger that had been propelling him along had left in a defeated rush, leaving him feeling more sad than anything else. And he didn't want to feel sad. God help him, he was *over* Sierra. He'd never loved her, after all—he'd desired her, yes. He'd wanted her very much.

But love? No. He'd never felt that and he had no intention of feeling it for anyone.

He slid his gaze towards her, saw the way her chest rose and fell under the baggy T-shirt. He could see the peaks of her nipples through the thin fabric, and desire arced through him. He still wanted her.

And did she want him? The question intrigued him and, even though he knew nothing would happen between them now, he realised he wanted to know the answer— very much.

There was only one way to find out. He reached for the salt, letting his arm brush across her breasts for one tantalising second. He heard her draw her breath in sharply and step back. When he glanced at her, he saw the colour flare into her face, her eyes widen before she quickly looked away.

Marco only just suppressed his smile as satisfaction surged through him. She wanted him. Seducing her would be easy…and such sweet revenge. But was that all he wanted from Sierra now? A moment's pleasure? The proof that she'd missed out? It felt petty and small, and more exposing of him than her.

And yet it would be so satisfying.

'What will you do with the estate?' She cleared her throat, her gaze flicking away from his as she stirred the pasta. 'Will you live here? Or sell it?'

'I haven't decided.' His thoughts of revenge were re-

placed by an uncomfortable flicker of guilt for taking Sierra's inheritance from her. Not that he'd actually wanted
to; Arturo had insisted, claiming Marco had been far more
of a son to him than Sierra had ever been a daughter. And,
in his self-righteous anger and hurt, Marco had relented.
Sierra had walked away from the family that had embraced
him. He'd believed she deserved what she'd got: nothing.

'Is there anything you want from the villa?' he asked.
'Or the *palazzo* in Palermo? Some heirlooms or pictures?'

She shook her head, her certainty shocking him even
though he knew it shouldn't. She'd turned her back on all
of it seven years ago. 'No. I don't want anything.'

'There's nothing?' he pressed. 'What about a photo-
graph of your parents? There's a wedding picture in the
front hall of the *palazzo*. It's lovely.' He watched her,
searching for some sign of softness, some relenting towards her family, towards him.

'No,' she said, and her voice was firm. 'I don't want
anything.'

They worked in silent tandem, preparing the simple
meal, and it wasn't until they were seated at the table in
the alcove with steaming plates of pasta that Sierra spoke
again.

'I always liked this spot. I ate breakfast here. The cook
was an old battleaxe who thought I should eat in the dining room but I couldn't bear it, with all the stuffy portraits
staring down at me so disapprovingly. I much preferred
it here.' She smiled, the gesture touched with sorrowful
whimsy.

Marco imagined her as a child sitting at the table, her
feet not even touching the floor. He imagined their daughter doing the same, and then abruptly banished the thought.
Dreams he'd once had of a proper family, a real life, and

now they were nothing but ashes and smoke. He'd never live here with Sierra or anyone.

'You can have the villa.' His voice came out abrupt, ungracious. Marco cleared his throat. 'I won't be using it. And it was your family home.'

She stared at him, her eyes wide. 'You're offering me the *villa*?'

He shrugged. 'Why shouldn't I? I didn't need any of your inheritance. The only thing I wanted was your father's shares in Rocci Enterprises.' Which gave him control of the empire he'd helped to build.

'Of course.' Her mouth curved in a mocking smile. 'That's why you wanted to marry me, after all.'

'What do you mean?' He stared at her in surprise, shocked by her assumption. 'Is that what you think? That I wanted to marry you only for personal gain?'

'Can you really deny it? What better way to move through the ranks than marry the boss's daughter?' She held his gaze and even though her voice was cool he saw pain in her eyes. Old, unforgotten pain, a remnant of long past emotion, and strangely it gratified him. So this was why she'd left—because she'd assumed he had been using her?

'I won't deny that there were some advantages to marrying you,' he began, and she let out a hard laugh.

'That's putting it mildly. You wouldn't have looked twice at me if my last name hadn't been Rocci.'

'That's not necessarily true. But I was introduced to you by your father. I always knew you were a Rocci.'

'And he stage-managed it all, didn't he? The whole reason he introduced you to me was to marry me off.'

Marco heard the bitterness in her voice and wondered at it. 'But surely you knew that.'

'Yes, I knew.' She shook her head, regret etched on her

fine-boned features. Marco laid down his knife and fork and stared at her hard.

'Then how can you object? Your father was concerned for your welfare. It made sense, assuming we got along, for him to encourage the match. He'd provide for his daughter and secure his business.'

'Which sounds positively medieval—'

'Not medieval,' Marco interjected. 'Sicilian, perhaps. He was an old-fashioned man, this is an old-fashioned country, with outdated ideas about some things. Trust me, I know.'

She looked up, the bitterness and regret sliding from her face, replaced by curiosity. 'Why do you say that? Why should you know better than another?'

He shouldn't have said that at all. He had no intention of telling Sierra about the shame of his parentage, the sorrow of his childhood. The past was best left forgotten, and he knew he could not stomach her pity. 'We've both encountered it, in different ways,' he answered with a shrug. 'But if you knew your father intended for us to marry, why do you fault me for it now?'

Sierra sighed and leaned back in her chair. 'I don't, not really.'

'But…' He shook his head, mystified and more than a little annoyed. 'I don't understand you, Sierra. Perhaps I never did.'

'I know.' She was quiet then, her face drawn in sorrowful lines. 'If it helps, I'm truly sorry for the way it all happened. If I'd had more courage, more clarity, I would have never let it get as far as it did. I would have never agreed to your proposal.'

And that was supposed to make him feel *better*? Marco's chest hurt with the pressure of holding back his anger and hurt. He was not going to show Sierra how her words wounded him. She saw their entire relationship as a mistake, an error of judgement. Until she hadn't come down the aisle, he'd been intending to spend the rest of his life with her. The difference in their experiences, their feelings, was too marked and painful for him to remark on it.

'I didn't intend to marry you simply because it was good business,' he finally managed, his voice level. He would not have her accuse him of being mercenary.

'I suppose it helped that I didn't have a face like an old boot,' Sierra returned before he could continue. 'And I was so biddable, wasn't I? So eager to please, practically fawning over you.' She shook her head in self-derision.

Marco cocked his head, surprise sweeping over him. 'Is that how you saw it?'

'That's how it was.'

He knew there was truth in what she said, but it hadn't been the whole truth. Yes, she'd been pretty and he'd been physically attracted to her. Overwhelmingly physically attracted to her, so his palms had itched to touch her softness, to feel her body yield to his. *And they still did.*

And yes, he'd liked how much she'd seemed to like him, how eager and admiring she'd been. What man wouldn't?

She'd been young and isolated, but so had he, even though he'd been almost thirty. Back then he hadn't had many, if any, people who looked up to him. He'd been a street rat from the dusty gutters of Palermo, a virtual orphan who had worked through half a dozen foster homes before he'd finally left at sixteen. No one had missed him.

Seeing Sierra Rocci look at him with stars in her eyes had felt *good*. Had made him feel part of something bigger than himself, and he'd craved that desperately. But Sierra made it sound as if he'd been calculating and cold, and it had never been like that for him.

'You are painting only part of the picture,' Marco finally said.

'Oh, I'm sure you felt an affection for me,' Sierra cut in. 'An amused tolerance, no doubt. But eventually you would have tired of me and I would have resented you. It would have been a disaster, like I said.'

He opened his mouth to object, to tell her what he'd hoped would have happened. That maybe they would have liked each other, grown closer. No, he hadn't loved her, hadn't wanted to love her. Hadn't wanted that much emotional risk. But he'd hoped for a good marriage. A real family.

She stared at him with challenge in her eyes and he closed his mouth. Why would he say all that now? Admit so much pathetic need? There was nothing between them now, no hope of any kind of future. Nothing but an intense physical awareness, and one he could use to his own ruthless advantage. Why shouldn't he? Why shouldn't he have Sierra Rocci in bed? Surely she wasn't the innocent she'd once been, and he could tell she desired him. Even if she didn't want to.

'Perhaps you're right,' he said tonelessly. 'In any case, you never gave us the opportunity to discover what might have happened. And, as you've said, it's all in the past.'

Sierra's breath left in a rush. 'Yes.' She sounded wary, as if she didn't trust his words, that he could be so forgiving.

'I'm glad you've realised that,' she said, her voice cool, and Marco inclined his head. 'I think I'll go to bed.' She rose gracefully and took her plate to the sink. Marco watched her go. 'It's been a long day and I have to get up early tomorrow for my flight.'

'Very well.'

She turned to him, uncertainty flashing in her eyes. 'Goodnight.'

Marco smiled fleetingly, letting his gaze rest on hers with intent, watching with satisfaction as her pupils flared and her breath hitched. 'Let me show you to your room.'

'It's not necessary—'

He rose from the table and strode towards her, his steps eating up the space in a few long strides. 'Oh,' he assured her with a smile that had become feral, predatory, 'but it is.'

CHAPTER FIVE

SHE COULDN'T SLEEP. Sierra lay in the double bed in the guest room Marco had shown her to a few hours ago and stared up at the ceiling. The rain drummed against the roof and the wind battered the shutters. And inside her a tangle of fear and desire left her feeling restless, uncertain.

She didn't think she'd been imagining the heightened sense of expectation as Marco had led her from the kitchen and up the sweeping marble staircase to the wing of guest bedrooms. She certainly hadn't been imagining the pulse of excitement she'd felt low in her belly when he'd taken her hand to guide her down the darkened corridor.

She hated how immediate and overwhelming her response to him was, and yet she told herself it was natural. Understandable. He was an attractive, virile man, and she'd responded to him before. She couldn't control the way he made her body feel, but she could certainly control her actions.

And so with effort she'd pulled her hand from his. The gesture seemed only to amuse him; he'd glanced back at her with a knowing smile, and Sierra had had the uncomfortable feeling that he knew exactly what she was thinking—and feeling.

But he hadn't acted on it. He'd shown her into the bedroom and she'd stood there, clearly *waiting*, while he'd turned on lights and checked that the shutters were bolted.

For an exquisite, excruciating second Sierra had thought he was going to do something. Kiss her. He'd stood in front of her, the lamplight creating a warm golden pool that bathed them both, and had looked at her. And she'd waited, ready, expectant...

If he'd kissed her then, she wouldn't have been able to resist. The realisation should have been shaming but she'd felt too much desire for that.

But Marco hadn't kissed her. His features had twisted in some emotion she couldn't discern, and then he'd simply said goodnight and left her alone. *Thank God.*

There was absolutely no reason whatsoever to feel disappointed about that.

Now Sierra rose from the bed, swinging her legs over so her bare feet hit the cold tiles. Music. Music was what she needed now. Music had always been both her solace and her inspiration. When she was playing the violin, she could soar far above all the petty worries and cruelties of her day-to-day life. But she didn't have her violin here; she'd left it in London.

Still, the villa had a music room with a piano. It was better than nothing. And she needed to escape from the din inside her own head, if only for a few minutes. Quietly, she crept from her bedroom and down the long darkened hallway. The house was silent save for the steady patter of rain, the distant rumble of thunder as the storm thankfully moved off.

Sierra tiptoed down the stairs, feeling her way through the dark, the moonless night not offering even a sliver of light. Finally, she found her way to the small music room with its French windows opening onto the terrace that was now awash in puddles.

She flicked on a single lamp, its warm glow creating a pool of light across the dusty ebony of grand piano. Gently she eased up the lid; the instrument was no doubt woefully out of tune. She quietly pressed a key and winced at the discordant sound.

Never mind. She sat at the piano and softly played the opening bars to Debussy's *Sarabande*, not wanting to wake Marco in one of the rooms above. Even with the piano out of tune, the music filled her, swept away her worries and regrets and left only light and sound in their wake. She closed her eyes, giving herself up to the piece, to the feeling. Forgetting, for a few needful moments, about her parents, her past, *Marco*.

She didn't know when she became aware that she wasn't alone. A prickling along her scalp, the nape of her neck. A shivery awareness that rippled through her and caused her to open her eyes.

Marco stood in the doorway of the music room, wearing only a pair of pyjama bottoms, his glorious chest bare, his gaze trained on her. Sierra's fingers stilled on the piano, plunging the room into an expectant silence.

'I didn't know you played piano.' His voice was low, husky with sleep, and it wove its sensual threads around her, ensnaring her.

'I don't, not really.' She put her hands in her lap, self-conscious and all too aware of Marco standing so near her, so bare and so beautiful. Every muscle of his chest was bronzed and perfectly sculpted; he looked like an ad for cologne or clothes or cars. Looking the way he did, she thought he could sell anyone anything. 'I had a few lessons,' Sierra continued stiltedly, 'but I'm mostly self-taught.'

'That's impressive.'

She shrugged, his surprising praise unnerving her. Having Marco standing here, wearing next to nothing, acting almost as if he admired her, sent her senses into hyperdrive and left her speechless.

'I never even knew you were musical.' He'd taken a step closer to her and she could feel the heat from his body. When she took a breath the musky male scent of him hit her nostrils and made her stomach clench. Hard.

'The violin is actually my chosen instrument, but it's not something I usually tell people. It's a private thing.' She forced herself to meet his sleepy, silvery gaze. She'd been a fool to come out of her bedroom tonight, and yet a distant part of her recognised she'd done it because she'd wanted this. Him. And even though desire was rushing through her in a torrent, both nerves and common sense made her back off. 'I'm sorry I disturbed you. I must have got carried away.' She half rose from the piano bench, halting inexplicably, pinned by his gaze.

'It sounded lovely.'

'The piano is out of tune.'

'Even so.'

He held her gaze, and inwardly Sierra quaked at how intent he looked. How utterly purposeful. So she wasn't even surprised when he reached a hand out and cupped her cheek, the pad of his thumb stroking the softness of her lower lip. Her breath caught in a gasp that lodged in her chest. Her heart started to pound. She'd been waiting for this, and even though she was afraid she knew she still wanted it.

'Almost,' he said softly, 'as lovely as you. Do you know how beautiful you are, Sierra? I've always thought that. You undid me, with your loveliness. I was caught from the moment I saw you, at your father's *palazzo*. Do you remember? You were standing in the drawing room, wearing a pink dress. You looked like a rose.'

She stared at him, shocked by how much he had admitted, how much he'd felt. 'I remember,' she whispered. Of course she remembered. She'd glimpsed him from the window, seen him gently stroke that silly cat, and felt her heart lift in both hope and desire. How quickly she'd fallen for him. How completely. Not in love, no, but in childish hope and longing. He'd overwhelmed her senses, even when she'd thought she'd been acting smart, playing safe.

'Do you remember when I kissed you?' Marco asked. His thumb pressed her lip gently, reminding her of how his lips had felt on hers. Hard, hot, soft, cool. Everything, all at once.

'Yes,' she managed in a shaky whisper. 'I remember.'

'You liked my kisses.' It was a statement, and he waited for her to refute it, confident that she couldn't. Sierra tried to look away but Marco held her gaze as if he were holding her face in place with his hands. He was that commanding, that forceful, and he hadn't even moved.

'You don't deny it.'

'No.' The word was drawn from her with helpless reluctance.

'You still like them, I think,' he said softly, and her silence condemned her. Slowly, inexorably, Marco drew her to him. She knew he was going to kiss her, and she knew she wanted him to. She also knew it was a bad idea, a *dangerous* idea, considering all that had—and hadn't—happened between them and yet she didn't resist.

His lips brushed hers once, twice. A shuddering sigh escaped her and she reached up to clutch his shoulders and steady herself. His skin felt hot and hard under her palms and she couldn't keep herself from smoothing her hands down his back, revelling in the feel of him. How could a man's skin feel so silky?

Marco's hands framed her face as he deepened the kiss,

his tongue sliding sweetly into her mouth as he tasted and explored her. He slid his hands from her face to her shoulders and then, wonderfully, to her breasts, cupping them as he had that day under the plane tree. She remembered how exciting it had felt, or at least she thought she had, but the reality of his touch now was so intense, so exquisite, she almost cried out as his thumbs brushed over her nipples. She hadn't remembered this, not enough.

'Marco.' His name came on a breath, and she didn't even know why she said it. Was she asking him to continue or telling him to stop?

He moved his mouth to her jaw, blazing kisses along her neck and collarbone as he slid his hand under her T-shirt and cupped her bare breast, the feel of his rough palm against her soft flesh, the gentle abrasion of it, making every nerve-ending blaze almost painfully to life. It was too much, and yet she wanted more.

'I want you.' He spoke hoarsely, firmly, declaring his intent. Sierra could only nod. He touched her chin with his fingers, forcing her to meet his blazing gaze. 'Say it. Say you want me, Sierra.'

'I want you,' she whispered, the words drawn from her, falling into the stillness, creating ripples.

Triumph blazed in his eyes as he pulled the T-shirt off her. She hadn't bothered with the tracksuit bottoms for pyjamas, so in one fluid movement she'd become naked. She sucked in a hard breath when he pulled her towards him, her breasts colliding and then crushed against his chest. The feel of their bare skin touching sent another tingling quiver of awareness shooting through her. Marco's hands were on her waist and then her hips as he fitted her against him. She could feel his arousal through the thin pyjama bottoms and it made her gasp. So many sensations all at once; she could barely acknowledge one before another came crashing over her.

Marco eased her back onto the piano bench, spreading her legs so he could stand between them. Her head fell back as he kissed his way from her collarbone to her breasts, and Sierra moaned as his tongue flicked across her sensitive flesh. She'd never realised you could feel this way, that a man could make you feel this way. He glanced up at her, his grey eyes blazing with triumph, and then he moved his head from her breasts to between her thighs and her breath came out in a shaky moan as he touched her centre.

'Oh.' She arched against his mouth, astonished at how sharp and intense the pleasure was, how consuming as his tongue found the very heart of her. *'Oh.'* She threaded her hands through his silky hair as her body arched helplessly against his mouth and his hands gripped her hips. It only took a few exquisite moments for her world to explode in glittering fragments around her and she cried out, one jagged note that echoed through the stillness of the villa.

She *really* had no idea.

She sagged against the piano as her body trembled with the aftershocks of her climax and Marco lifted his head to gaze at her with blatant—and smug—satisfaction. Re-alisation thudded sickly through her; his look said it all. He'd been trying to prove something, and he'd just proved it—in spades.

Shakily, colour rushing to her face, Sierra pushed her tangle of hair from her hot cheeks and closed her legs, pushing him away from her. The intensity of the moment had splintered, leaving her feeling raw and exposed. Wounded and ashamed. She'd been so wanton, so shame-less, and Marco had been utterly in control. *As always.*

'Now at least you know a little of what you've missed,' he said and her mouth opened on a soundless gasp.

'You've proved your point, then, I suppose,' she managed and on shaking legs she grabbed her T-shirt and rushed from the room.

Marco stalked upstairs, his whole body throbbing with unfulfilled desire—and worse, regret. He'd behaved like a cad. A heartless, cruel cad. And he needed an icy-cold shower. Swearing under his breath, he strode into his bedroom and went straight to the en suite bathroom, turning the cold on full blast. He stepped beneath the needling spray, sucking in a hard breath as the icy water hit his skin and chilled him right through. And even then he couldn't quench the fire that raged in his veins, heated his blood, born of both shame and lust.

He'd wanted her so much, more than he'd ever wanted another woman. More than he'd ever thought possible. The sweetness of her response, the *innocence* of it... Marco braced his hands against the shower stall. He could almost believe she was still untouched. She'd seemed so surprised by everything, so enthralled. And when she'd fallen to pieces beneath his mouth...

Forcefully he pushed the memory away. The last thing he needed now was to remember how that had felt. Better to remember the sudden look of uncertainty on her face, of shame. The realisation that he'd been low enough to exact some kind of revenge, using her body against her. Forcing her to respond to him, even though she'd once rejected him.

He'd been tempted to seduce her, yes, and he could have had her earlier, when he'd shown her to her bedroom. He'd seen the uncertainty and desire in her eyes, how she had hesitated. But he'd resisted the temptation, had told himself he was better than that.

Apparently he wasn't.

His body numb with cold, his blood still hot, Marco

turned off the shower and wrapped a towel around his hips. Sleep would not come for him tonight, not when too many emotions still churned through him. He went to his laptop instead, powered it up and prepared to work.

By dawn his eyes were gritty, his body aching, but at least the rain had stopped. Marco stood at the window and gazed out at the rain-washed gardens. The once manicured lawns and groomed beds were a wild tangle of shrubs and trees; he hadn't looked after the estate in the last few years, when Arturo had been too ill to do so himself. He'd hire a gardener to clean it up before he sold it. He didn't want to have anything more to do with the place.

When he came downstairs Sierra was already in the kitchen, dressed in the silk blouse and pencil skirt she'd worn yesterday. Both were creased but dry; she'd put her hair back up in its sleek chignon and all of it felt like armour, a way to protect herself against him.

Marco hesitated in the doorway, wondering whether to mention last night. What would he even say? In any case Sierra looked as if she wanted to pretend it hadn't happened, and maybe that was best.

'We should get on the road if your flight is this afternoon.'

'We?' She shook her head firmly. 'I'll drive myself.'

'The mountain roads still aren't passable, and your rental car looks like little more than a tin can on wheels,' Marco dismissed. 'I'll drive you. My car can handle the flooding.'

'But what about my rental…?'

'I'll have someone pick it up and deliver it to the agency. It's not a problem.'

She licked her lips, her eyes wide, her expression more than a little panicked. 'But…'

'It makes sense, Sierra. And, trust me, you don't have

to worry about some kind of repeat of last night. I don't intend to touch you ever again.' He hadn't meant to sound quite so harsh, but he saw the surprised hurt flicker in her eyes before she looked away.

'And I have no intention of letting you touch me ever again.'

He was almost tempted to prove her wrong, but he resisted the impulse. The sooner Sierra was out of his life, the better. 'It seems we're agreed, then. Now, we should get ready to go.' Marco grabbed his keys and switched off the lights before ushering Sierra out of the kitchen. He followed her, locking the villa behind him, and then opened the passenger door to his SUV. As Sierra slid inside the car he breathed in her lemony scent, and his gut tightened. It was going to be a long three hours.

They drove in silence down the sweeping drive, the villa's gates closing silently behind them. Sierra let out a sigh of relief as Marco turned onto the mountain road.

'You're glad to leave?'

'Not glad, exactly,' she answered. 'But memories can be…difficult.'

He couldn't argue with that. He had a truckload of difficult memories, from his father's retreat from his life, to his mother leaving him at the door of an orphanage run by monks when he was ten years old, to the slew of foster homes he'd bounced through, to the endless moment when he'd stood at the front of the church, the smile slipping from his face as Arturo came down the aisle, his face set in extraordinarily grim lines.

Sierra was staring out of the window; it was as if she'd dismissed him entirely. As he would dismiss her. For better or worse, last night's episode would serve as a line drawn across the past. Perhaps he had evened the score between them. In any case, his tie to Sierra Rocci was cut—firmly and for ever.

Setting his jaw, Marco stared straight ahead as he drove in silence all the way to Palermo.

CHAPTER SIX

'You need Sierra Rocci.'

Marco swivelled around in his chair to gaze out of the window at Palermo's business district as everything in him resisted that flatly spoken statement. 'I've been Arturo's right-hand man for nearly ten years. I don't need her.'

Paolo Conti, his second-in-command and closest confidant, sighed. 'I'm afraid you do, Marco. The board isn't happy without a Rocci to front the business, at least at first. And with the hotel opening in New York in a few weeks...'

'What about it? Everything is going according to plan.' He'd overseen the work on Rocci Enterprises' first hotel in North America himself; it had been his idea to expand, and to take the exclusive chain of hotels in a new direction. His credibility as CEO rested on The Rocci New York succeeding.

'That's true,' Paolo replied, 'but in the seventy years of Rocci Enterprises, a Rocci has always headed the board.'

'Things change.'

'Yes,' Paolo agreed patiently, running his hand through his silver hair, 'but for the last seventy years a Rocci has opened each hotel. Palermo, Rome, Paris, Madrid, London, Berlin.' He ticked them off on his fingers. 'A Rocci at every one.'

'I know.' He'd seen a few of the grand openings himself. He'd started work for Rocci Enterprises when he was sixteen years old, as a bellboy at the hotel in Palermo. He'd seen Sierra walking with her parents up the pink marble steps to eat in the hotel's luxurious dining room. He'd watched her walk so daintily, her hands held by both her mother and father. The perfect family.

'Change is a part of life,' Marco dismissed, 'and Arturo Rocci willed his shares to me. The board—and the public—will simply have to adjust.' It had been nearly a month since he'd left Sierra at the Palermo airport. Four weeks since he'd watched her walk away from him and told himself he was glad, even as he felt the old injustice burn. She hadn't looked back.

He wasn't angry with her any more, but he didn't know what he felt. Whatever emotion raged through him didn't feel good.

'It's not that simple, Marco,' Paolo said. He'd been with Rocci Enterprises for decades, always quietly serving and guiding. As Arturo had become more and more ill, Marco had relied increasingly on Paolo's help and wisdom.

'It can be,' he insisted.

'If the board feels there is too much separation from the Rocci name and values, they might hold a vote of no confidence.'

Marco tensed. 'I've been with this company for over ten years. And I hold the controlling shares.'

'The board needs to see you in public, acting as CEO. They need to believe in you.'

'Fine. I'll appear at any number of events.'

'With a Rocci,' Paolo clarified. 'And, as you know, Sierra is the only Rocci left.' Arturo's brother, a bachelor, had died a dozen years ago, his parents before then. 'There needs to be a smooth transition,' Paolo insisted. 'For the board *and* the public. Arturo wasn't able to manage it while he was alive—'

'He was ill.'

'I know. I'm sure he would have addressed this himself if he could have.'

But Arturo hadn't made Marco the beneficiary of his will until the very end. Marco suspected the old man had been hoping for Sierra to come back, to keep the business in the family. Restlessly, Marco rose from his chair and paced his office. Damn it, he'd given his life to Rocci Enterprises. He could still remember the sense of incredulous joy he'd had when Arturo had moved him from hefting suitcases to working in an office. Arturo Rocci had seen his potential and helped him to rise. And he'd paid his mentor back tenfold, by increasing Rocci Enterprises' revenue and expanding its business concerns. But he feared that all his board saw was a street rat from Palermo's gutters who had got ideas far above his station.

Sighing, he sank back into his chair. He could see the sense in what Paolo was saying. A smooth transition from him being the second-in-command who worked invisibly behind the scenes to being the public face of Rocci Enterprises. All it would take was a few key appearances, some stage-managed events…with Sierra.

Considering how they'd parted, he doubted Sierra Rocci was going to want to help him out in any fashion. He might not be angry with her any more, but she could very well still harbour a grudge for his ruthless semiseduction of her at the villa. Sighing, he closed his eyes and rubbed his temples, fighting off the tension headache that felt like a band of iron encircling his head.

He didn't want to need Sierra. He certainly didn't want to go begging for favours. But Rocci Enterprises meant everything to him. He couldn't afford to risk its well-being.

'Well?' Paolo asked. 'Do you think Sierra Rocci will agree? I know the two of you have a history…' He paused delicately, and Marco opened his eyes.

'I'll make her agree,' he stated flatly. Already his mind was racing through the possibilities. How could he get Sierra to come to New York? She'd accused him of being manipulative seven years ago, of engaging her affections so he could secure his position with Rocci Enterprises. She'd been wrong then, or at least that hadn't been the whole truth. But now it would be.

Marco's mouth curved coldly. 'Don't worry,' he told Paolo. 'I know how to handle her.'

'Play it again please, Chloe.'

Sierra shifted in her hard chair as her pupil sawed her way through 'Twinkle, Twinkle, Little Star' for the third time. Sierra tried not to wince. She loved her job tutoring children in music for a variety of after-school clubs, but it wasn't always easy on the ears.

Her mind drifted, as it had these last few weeks, to Marco Ferranti. It irritated and unnerved her that he was so often in her thoughts; the passionate interlude in the music room had haunted her dreams and left her aching with both desire and shame.

There was so much she didn't understand about Marco. He seemed like a tangle of unsettling contradictions: his anger at her abandonment of him seven years ago, and then the sudden moments of generosity and even tenderness that he'd shown her. Which was the real man? Which was the act? And why on earth was she still thinking about him?

'Miss Rocci?'

Sierra's unfocused gaze settled on the little girl in front of her. 'Yes, Chloe?'

'I finished.'

'Yes, of course you did,' Sierra murmured. 'Well done.' She leafed through the music she'd brought before selecting another piece. 'Why don't you try this one now that you've managed "Twinkle, Twinkle" so well?'

An hour later Sierra packed up her things and headed out of the school where she'd been running music lessons. It had taken a few years, but she'd managed to build up a regular business, offering lessons to schoolchildren across London's schools.

After her tumultuous and panicked flight from Sicily, she'd found her mother's friend Mary Bertram living in London; she'd moved house but, with the help of the internet, Sierra had managed to track her down. Mary had sheltered her, helped her find her feet along with her first job. She'd died three years ago, and Sierra had felt as if she'd lost another mother.

Outside the school, she started down the pavement towards the Tube station, the midsummer evening sultry and warm. People were spilling out of houses and offices, laughing as they slung bags over their shoulders and made plans for the pub.

Sierra regarded them with a slight pang of envy. She'd never been able to make friends easily; her isolated childhood and her innate quietness had made it difficult. Her job was isolated, too, although she'd become friendly with a few of the other extracurricular teachers at various schools. But in the seven years she'd lived in London, no one had got close. She'd never had a lover or even a boyfriend, nothing more than a handful of dates that had gone nowhere.

'Hello, Sierra.'

Sierra came to a shocked halt as Marco Ferranti stepped out in front of her. Her mouth opened soundlessly; she felt as if she'd conjured him from thin air, from her lonely thoughts. He quirked an eyebrow, his mouth curving in the gentle quirk of a smile she recognised from seven years ago.

'What…what are you doing here?' she finally managed.

'Looking for you.'

A thrill of illicit pleasure as well as of apprehension shivered through her. He'd come to London just for her? 'How did you know where I was?'

He shrugged, the movement assured, elegant. 'Information is always easy to find.'

And just like that she was unnerved again, realising once more how little she knew him, the real him. How powerful he was. 'I don't know why you'd want to talk to me, Marco.'

'Is there somewhere private we could go?'

She glanced around the busy city street and shrugged. 'Not really.'

'Then let me find a place.' Marco slid his phone from the pocket of his suit jacket and thumbed a few buttons. Within seconds he was issuing instructions and then he returned his phone to his pocket and put his hand on the small of Sierra's back, where it rested enticingly, his palm warm through the thin fabric of her summer blouse. 'I've found a place.'

'Just like that?' Sierra hadn't heard what he'd said into the phone; his Italian had been low and rapid, inaudible over the sounds of traffic.

'Just like that,' Marco answered with a smile and guided her down the street, his hand never leaving her back.

A few minutes later they were entering a wine bar with plush velvet sofas and tables of polished ebony and teak. Sierra gaped to see a sofa in a private alcove already prepared for them, a bottle of red wine opened and breathing next to two crystal wine glasses.

'Some service,' she remarked shakily.

'As a Rocci, you must be used to such service,' Marco replied. He gestured for her to sit down while he poured the wine.

'Perhaps, but it's been a while.' In the seven years since she'd come to London she'd lived on little more than a pittance. She rented a tiny flat in Clapham and she bought everything second-hand. The days of luxury and privilege as Arturo Rocci's daughter were long over.

As she sank into the velvet sofa and watched Marco pour her a glass of wine, Sierra couldn't help but enjoy the moment. Even if Marco's presence overwhelmed and unnerved her. She had no idea why he'd come to London to find her, or what he could possibly want.

'Here.' He pressed a glass of wine into her hand and she took a much-needed sip.

'What do you want from me?' she asked, and then steeled herself for his answer.

Whatever they were, Marco wasn't going to reveal his intentions so easily. 'I didn't realise you were a music teacher.'

So he'd done some digging. She took another sip of wine. 'I teach children in after-school clubs.'

'And you play the piano and violin yourself.'

'Only in private.' Her cheeks heated as Marco's knowing gaze locked with hers. She knew they were both remembering the last time she'd played, and just how private it had been.

'I'd like to hear you play the violin.' His gaze seemed to caress her, and she felt goosebumps rise on her arms as a familiar ache started in her centre. 'I'd like you to play it for me.' His voice was low, sensuous, his gaze never leaving hers, his words making images and ideas leap into her mind in a vivid and erotic montage.

Sierra shook her head slowly, forcing the feelings back. 'Why are you acting this way, Marco?'

He took a sip of wine, one eyebrow arched. 'What way?'

'Like…like a lover,' she blurted, and then blushed. 'The last time we saw each other you seemed glad to be shot of me.'

'And I must confess you seemed likewise.'

'Considering the circumstances, not to mention our history, yes.'

'I'm sorry for the way I acted,' Marco said abruptly. His gaze was still locked on hers, his expression intent. 'In the music room. When I made love to you. I was trying to prove you still desired me and it was a petty, stupid thing to do. I'm sorry.' His lips curved in a tiny smile. 'Even if it seemed you enjoyed it.'

His words were gently teasing, and they made her blush all the more. She had no idea how to respond.

'Thank you,' she finally muttered. 'For your apology. But I still don't know why you're here.'

Marco shifted in his seat, his powerful thigh brushing her leg. The contact sent sizzling arrows of remembered sensation firing through her, and Sierra only just resisted pulling away. She wouldn't show him how much he affected her. In any case, he undoubtedly already knew.

'I've been thinking about you, Sierra.' His voice flowed over like her melted chocolate, warm and liquid, enticing but also a way to drown. 'A lot.'

Her mouth had dried, her lungs emptying of air, and yet suspicion and doubt still took hold of her heart. She shook her head slowly. 'Marco…'

'I've been thinking that it's unfair you didn't receive anything from your father's will.'

The abrupt reality check felt like falling flat on her face. Left her breathless, smarting. Of course he wasn't thinking about her *that* way. She shouldn't even want to be thinking of him *that* way. Good grief, where was her backbone? Her resolve? She'd spent the last seven years telling herself she'd done the right thing in walking away from this man, and now she was panting and dreaming like some lovesick teenager.

'I don't care about my father's will.'

'You should. You had a birthright, Sierra.'

'Even though I walked away from my family? In di Santis's office you seemed to think I was getting exactly what I deserved. Almost nothing.' She hadn't cared about her father's inheritance, but Marco's smug triumph had rankled. More than rankled, if she was honest. It had hurt.

'I was angry,' Marco admitted quietly. 'I'm sorry.'

So many apologies. She didn't know what to do with them. She didn't entirely trust them—or him. And her own feelings were cartwheeling all over the place, which made sounding and feeling logical pretty difficult. 'It's all in the past, Marco. Let's leave it there.'

'I think you should have a part in Rocci Enterprises.'

She drew back, truly startled. If anything, she'd been expecting him to offer her the villa again, or perhaps some family heirlooms she had no need for. Not her father's business. 'I've never had a part in Rocci Enterprises.' Her father had been very much of the persuasion that women didn't need to be involved in business. She'd left school at sixteen at her father's behest.

'A new hotel is opening in New York City,' Marco continued as if she hadn't spoken. 'It will be the most luxurious Rocci hotel yet, and I think you should be there. You deserve to be there.'

'In New York?' She stared at him in disbelief.

'You opened four hotels before you were nineteen,'

Marco reminded her. 'People are used to seeing a Rocci cut the ribbon. You should be the one to do it.'

'I had nothing to do with that hotel, or any of them.' She was filled with sudden and utter revulsion at the thought of opening one of her father's hotels. Playing happy families, and this time from the grave. How many times had she smiled and curtsied for the crowds, how many times had her mother waved, wearing a long-sleeved dress to hide the bruises? She had no desire whatsoever to revisit those memories or play that part again. 'I appreciate your consideration,' she said stiffly, 'but I don't need to open the hotel. I have no wish to.' Some of her distaste must have shown on her face because Marco frowned.

'Why not?'

Sierra hesitated, stalling for time by taking a sip of wine. She was still hesitant to tell Marco the truth of her father, her family, because she didn't think he'd believe her and even if he did she didn't want his pity. It was shaming to admit she'd allow herself to be abused and used for so long, even if she'd only been a child. And if he didn't believe her? If he accused her of lying or exaggerating to sully her father's name? Or maybe he *would* believe her, and think her father had been justified. Maybe he countenanced a little rough handling. The truth was, she had no idea what his response would be and she had no intention of finding out.

'Sierra?' He leaned forward, covering her hand with his own. She realised she was trembling and she strove for control.

'Like I said, the past is in the past, Marco. I don't need to be part of Rocci Enterprises. I left it behind when I left Sicily.' She forced a smile, small and polite, definitely strained. 'But, as I said, thank you for thinking of me.'

His hand still rested on hers; it felt warm and strong.

Comforting, even if it shouldn't be. Even if she still didn't understand or trust this man. She didn't pull away.

Confused frustration surged through him as Marco gazed at Sierra, tried to figure out what she was thinking. His magnanimous approach had clearly failed. He'd hoped that Sierra would embrace his suggestion, that she'd be glad to have a chance to mend a few bridges, be a Rocci again. More fool him.

He sat back, letting go of her hand, noticing the loss even as his mind raced for another way forward. 'You don't seem to bear much good will for Rocci Enterprises,' he remarked, 'even though you were obviously close to your family at one time.'

Her mouth twisted. 'I don't feel anything for Rocci Enterprises,' she said flatly. 'I was never part of it.'

'You were at every hotel opening—'

'For show.' She turned away, her expression closing, her gaze downcast so he could see her blond lashes fanning her cheeks.

'For show?' He disliked the thought instinctively. 'It looked real to me.'

'It was meant to.'

'What are you saying? I know your parents loved you very much, Sierra. I saw how they reacted when you left. They were devastated, both of them. Your father couldn't speak of you without tears coming into his eyes. And you never even wrote them a letter to say you were safe.' His voice throbbed with intensity, with accusation, and Sierra noticed. Her gaze narrowed and her lips pursed.

'You don't think my father could have found me if he wanted?'

'Of course he could have. He was a very powerful man.'

'So why do you think he didn't?'

Marco hesitated, trying to assess Sierra's tone, her mood. 'Sierra,' he said finally, 'I am under no illusions about your father. He was a proud and sometimes ruthless man, but he was honourable. *Good.*' Sierra pressed her lips together and said nothing. 'You hurt him very much by leaving. Even if he'd never admit it.'

'Of course.' She shook her head. 'Why did you ask me to come to New York?' she said. 'Really?'

Unease spiked in his gut. 'What do you mean?'

'I mean you're not telling me the truth. Not the whole truth,' she amended when he opened his mouth to object. 'Just like always. This isn't some act of chivalry, is it, Marco? It isn't some benevolent impulse you've had out of the goodness of your heart.' She shook her head slowly. 'I almost bought it. I almost bought the whole act, because I was almost so stupid. Again.'

'*Again?*'

'I trusted you seven years ago—'

'I wasn't the one who betrayed a trust,' Marco snapped.

Sierra leaned forward, her eyes glittering icy-blue now, two slits of arctic rage. 'And you say you're not angry any more? Why are you here? Why am *I* here?' She folded her arms, levelling him with her glare. 'What do you really want from me?'

CHAPTER SEVEN

SHE COULDN'T BELIEVE how gullible she'd been—*again*. Wanting to believe the best of Marco Ferranti. Wanting, instinctively, to trust him. Hadn't she learned *anything*? No matter how kind he could seem, he'd been her father's apprentice for ten years. He'd wanted to marry her to further his business interests. And yet some part of her still wanted him to be kind.

'Well?' she demanded. 'Have I actually managed to render you speechless?'

'You're jumping to conclusions,' Marco said, an edge entering his voice. The charm was gone, dropped like the flimsy, false mask it was. She knew how it went. Fear spiked through her and she tamped it down. She would be no man's punching bag, emotional or physical, again.

'Then why don't you try being honest?'

'I was being honest. I do think you should have some part in Rocci Enterprises. In fact, if you'd given me a chance, I would have told you I'm prepared to give you most of your inheritance back.' He eyed her coolly, as if waiting for her to trip over herself with gratitude.

'That's very big of you,' she answered, sarcasm spiking her voice. 'You're *prepared* to give me *most*. That's so very, very noble.'

Marco's lip curled. 'You want more?'

'I don't want anything but the truth. Stop trying to manipulate me. Just tell me what you want.'

A muscle ticked in his jaw as their gazes clashed. Even with the anger simmering between them, Sierra felt an unwelcome kick of desire. A sudden sharp memory of the way he'd plundered her mouth, her body…and how good it had felt.

She saw an answering spark of awareness in Marco's eyes and knew he was remembering, too.

Good grief, what was *wrong* with her? How could she still want a man whom she couldn't trust, didn't like? Why did she have to have this intense physical reaction to him?

'I'm still waiting,' she snapped.

'Having you open the New York hotel is of some benefit to me, too,' Marco finally bit out. 'Fine, I'll admit it. The public would like to see a Rocci cut the damn ribbon.'

She sat back against the sofa, strangely deflated by his admission. 'So you were trying to make it seem like you were being nice. Thoughtful. When really you just wanted me to come for your sake.'

'For the company's sake. You might have no great interest in Rocci Enterprises, but do you want to see it fail? Seventy years of history, Sierra, and most of my life.'

'I don't care about Rocci Enterprises,' she said flatly. 'I don't care if it fails.'

'You don't care about your family's livelihood?'

'The only family left is me, and I make my own living,' she retorted. 'Stop trying to guilt me into this.'

'What about the livelihood of all the employees? Five hundred people are going to be employed by Rocci New York. If the hotel fails—'

'The hotel is not going to *fail* if I'm not there,' Sierra declared. 'My father has opened several hotels in the last seven years. I haven't been at any of them. I'm not needed, Marco.'

'As you pointed out yourself, you're the only Rocci left and people want to see you.' He paused. 'The board wants to see you.'

'Ah.' It was starting to make more sense now. 'Your job is in jeopardy.'

His mouth tightened. 'I have the controlling shares of the company.'

'But if you lose the confidence of the board as well as the public?' She shook her head. 'It won't look good.'

Fury flared in his eyes and Sierra felt an answering alarm. She was baiting him, and why? Because she was angry. She was furious and hurt that he'd been using her. Again. And she'd almost let him.

'I'm leaving.' She shoved her wine glass onto the coffee table with a clatter and rose from the sofa, grabbing her bag. 'Thanks for the drink,' she tossed over her shoulder, and then she strode from the wine bar.

She was halfway down the street, her heels clicking loudly on the pavement, when she heard his voice from behind.

'I need you, Sierra. I admit it.'

She slowed but didn't stop. Was this simply more manipulation?

'I don't want to need you, God knows.' There was a note in his voice that she hadn't heard before, a weary defeat that touched her even though she knew it shouldn't. 'I don't want to be at your mercy. I was once before and it didn't feel all that great.'

She turned around slowly, shocked when she saw him standing there, his expression unguarded and open in a way she'd never seen before.

'When were you at my mercy?'

'When I stood at the front of the church and waited for you to show up at our wedding.' He took a step towards her. People had been streaming past them but now a few slowed, curious about the drama that was being enacted on a London street. 'Why would you help me?' he asked. 'I didn't feel I could simply ask. I didn't want to simply ask, because I didn't want to be refused. Rejected.' His mouth twisted in a grimace and Sierra realised how hard this was for him. This—here, now—was real honesty. 'Again.'

'Marco…'

'I poured my life into Rocci Enterprises,' he said, his voice low and intense. 'Everything I had. I've worked for the company since I was sixteen. I started as a bellboy, which is something you probably didn't know.'

'A bellboy…' Sierra shook her head. She'd assumed Marco had come in on the executive level. She'd never asked, and he'd never spoken about his history, his background or his family. A painful reminder of how little she knew about him.

'Your father saw my potential and promoted me. He treated me like a son from the beginning. And I gave everything in return. Everything.'

'I know you did.' And Marco's unwavering loyalty was, Sierra surmised, why her father had chosen him in the first place, both as business associate and prospective son-in-law. Because her father had wanted someone who would forever be in his debt.

Marco closed his eyes briefly. 'The company is my family, my life. Losing it…' His voice choked and he ran a hand through his hair. 'I can't bear the thought of it. So I am sorry I tried to manipulate you. I apologise for not being honest. But you have my life in your hands, Sierra, whether you want to or not. I know you bear no love or even affection for me, and I accept that my behaviour recently hasn't deserved it. But all I have left, all I can do now, is to throw myself on your mercy.' His gaze met hers, bleak, even hopeless. 'Not a position I ever wanted to be in, and yet here I am.'

He hadn't meant to say all of that. He'd come into this meeting wanting to keep his pride intact, and instead he'd had everything stripped away. Revealed. He might as well be standing by the damned altar, waiting for his bride. If she refused him now...

He couldn't tell what she was thinking or feeling. She'd cloaked herself in that cool composure he'd once admired. He waited, breath held, having no idea what he could say or do if she told him *no*. If she walked away. Then she spoke.

'I'll go to New York,' she said. 'And I'll open the hotel.'

Relief poured through him, made him nearly sag with the force of it. 'Thank you.'

She nodded stiffly. 'When is it?'

'In two weeks.'

'You can forward me the details,' she said, and for a second her expression wobbled, almost as if she was going to cry. Then she nodded her farewell and turned and walked down the street, away from him.

Sierra peeked out of the window of her ground floor flat at the sleek black limo that had just pulled up to the kerb. Marco had said he would send a car, and she supposed she shouldn't be surprised that it was a limo.

But she was surprised when he stepped out, looking as devastatingly sexy as ever in a crisply tailored navy blue suit. She'd assumed she would meet him at the airport. Apparently Marco had other ideas.

Nervously, she straightened the pale grey sheath dress

she'd chosen for travel. She didn't have too many fancy clothes and after she'd agreed to Marco's suggestion, out on the street, she'd realised she didn't have anything to wear to the ball on the night of the hotel's opening. She'd used some of her paltry savings to buy a second-hand dress at a charity shop and hoped that in the dim lighting no one would notice the fraying along the hem.

Marco rapped on the front door and, taking a deep breath, Sierra willed her shoulders back and went to answer it.

'Hello, Sierra.' His voice felt like a fist plunging inside her soul. Ever since she'd seen him out on that street, admitting everything, being honest and open, she'd been plagued by doubts, filled with hope. *Here* finally was the man she could trust and like. The man she'd glimpsed seven years ago. And she didn't know whether to be glad or fearful of the fact. In some ways it had been easier, simpler, to hate Marco Ferranti.

'You're ready?' His gaze swept over her in one swift assessment as she nodded.

'Yes, I'll just fetch my case.'

'I'll get it.' He shouldered past her so she could breathe in the scent of his aftershave and hefted her single suitcase easily. 'This is all you're bringing?'

'I don't need much.'

He frowned, his straight eyebrows drawing together as his gaze moved around the tiny sitting room with its shabby sofa and rickety chairs. She'd tried to make it homely with some throws and framed posters, but it was a far cry from the luxury Marco was used to. 'What about a hanging case, for your evening clothes?'

She thought of the second-hand dress folded in her suitcase. 'It's fine.'

Marco didn't answer; he just took her suitcase and

walked out of the flat. Sierra expelled a shaky breath and then followed him, locking the door behind her.

In the two weeks since she'd agreed to accompany Marco to New York, she'd questioned her decision many times. Wondered why on earth she was entangling herself with Marco again, when things between them were complicated enough. Surely it would be better, or at least easier, to walk away for good. Draw a final line across the past.

But there on the street she'd seen Marco as she'd never seen him before. She'd seen him being open and honest, *vulnerable*, and she'd believed him. For once suspicion hadn't hardened her heart or doubt clouded her mind. She'd known Marco was speaking the truth even when he didn't want to, when it made him feel weak.

And so she'd said yes.

And not just because he'd been so honest, Sierra knew. It was more complicated than that. Because she felt she owed him something, after the way she'd walked away seven years ago. And, if she was as honest as he had been, because she wanted to see him again. And that was very dangerous thinking.

The driver of the limo took her suitcase from Marco and stowed it in the back as Marco opened the door and ushered her inside the car.

Sierra slid inside the limo, one hand smoothing across one of the sumptuous leather seats that faced each other. She scooted to the far side as Marco climbed inside, and suddenly the huge limo with its leather sofa-like seats and coffee table seemed very small.

It was going to be a long three days. An exciting three days. Maybe that was another reason she'd agreed; as much as she liked her life in London, it was quiet and unassuming. The thought of spending three days in luxury in New

York, three days with Marco, was a heady one. Even if it
shouldn't be.

The door closed and Marco settled in the seat across
from her, stretching his legs out so his knee nudged hers.
Sierra didn't move, not wanting to be obvious about how
much he affected her. Just that little nudge sent her pulse
skyrocketing, although maybe it was everything all at once
that was affecting her: the limo, the scent of his aftershave, the real and magnetic presence of the man oppo-
site her, and the fact that she'd be spending the next three
days with him.

She looked out of the window, afraid all her apprehension and excitement would be visible on her face.

'Are you all right?'

She turned back, startled and a little embarrassed. 'Yes,
I'm fine.'

'Have some water.' He handed her a bottle of water and
after a moment Sierra uncapped it and took a drink, conscious of Marco's eyes on her as she swallowed. 'I do appreciate you agreeing to do this,' he said quietly.

She lowered the bottle to look at him; his expression
was shuttered, neutral, all the openness and honesty he'd
shown two weeks ago tucked safely away. 'It's no hard-
ship, spending a few days in New York,' she said.

'You seemed quite opposed to the idea initially.'

She sighed and screwed the cap back on the bottle of
water. 'Revisiting everything in the past has been hard. I
want to move on with my life.'

'After this you can, I promise. I won't bother you again,
Sierra.'

Which should make her feel relieved rather than disappointed. Not trusting herself to speak, Sierra just nodded.

They kept the conversation light after that, speaking
only of innocuous subjects: travel and food and films. By

the time they reached the airport Sierra was starting to feel more relaxed, although her nerves jumped to alert when Marco took her arm as they left the limo.

He led her through the crowds, bypassing the queue at check-in for private VIP service.

'This is the life,' Sierra teased as they settled in the private lounge and a waiter brought a bottle of champagne and two flutes. 'Are we celebrating?'

'The opening of The Rocci New York,' Marco answered easily. 'Surely you've travelled VIP before?'

She shook her head. 'No, I've hardly travelled at all. Going to London was the first time I'd left the mainland of Europe.'

'Was it?' Marco frowned, clearly surprised by this information, and Sierra wondered just how rosy a view he had of her family life. Had he not realised how her father had tucked his family away, bringing them out only when necessary? But she didn't want to dwell on the past and neither, it seemed, did Marco, for after the waiter had popped the cork on the champagne and poured them both glasses, he asked, 'So how did you get into teaching in London?'

'I volunteered at first, and took some lessons myself. It started small—I took a slot at an after-school club and then word spread and more schools asked.' She shrugged. 'I'm not grooming too many world-class musicians, but I enjoy it and I think the children do, as well.'

'And you like London?'

'Yes. It's different, of course, and I could do without the rain, but...' She shrugged and took a sip of champagne, enjoying the way the bubbles zinged through her. 'It's become home.'

'You've made friends?' The innocuous lilt to his voice belied the sudden intensity she saw spark in his eyes. What was he really asking?

'I've made a few. Some teachers, a few neighbours.' She shrugged. 'I'm used to being solitary.'

'Are you? Why?'

'I spent most of my childhood in the mountains or at convent school. Company was scarce.'

'I suppose your father was strict and old-fashioned about that kind of thing.'

Her stomach tightened, memory clenching inside her. 'You could say that.'

'But he had a good heart. He always wanted the best for you.'

Sierra didn't reply. Couldn't. Marco sounded so sincere, so sure. How could she refute what he said? Now seemed neither the time nor the place. 'And for you,' she said after a moment, when she trusted her voice to sound measured and mild. 'He loved you like a son. More than I ever even realised.'

Marco nodded, his expression sombre, the corners of his mouth pulled down. 'He was like a father to me. Better than my own father.'

Curiosity sharpened inside her. 'Why? What was your own father like?'

He hesitated, his glass halfway to his lips, his mouth now a hard line. 'I don't really know. He was out of my life by the time I was seven years old.'

'He was? I'm sorry.' She paused, feeling her way through the sudden minefield of their conversation. It was obvious from his narrowed eyes and his tense shoulders, that Marco didn't like talking about his past. And yet Sierra wanted to know. 'I've realised how little I knew about you. Your childhood, your family.'

'That's because they're not worth knowing.'

'What happened to your father when you were seven?'

He was silent for a moment, marshalling his thoughts,

and Sierra waited. 'I'm illegitimate,' he finally stated flatly. 'My mother was a chambermaid at one of the hotels in Palermo—not The Rocci,' he clarified with a small, hard smile. 'My father was an executive at the hotel. Married, of course. They had an affair, and my mother became pregnant. That old story.' He shrugged dismissively, as if he wasn't going to say anything more.

'And then what happened?' Sierra asked after a moment.

'My mother had me, and my father set her up in a dingy flat in one of Palermo's slums. Gave her enough to live on—just. He'd visit us on occasion, a few times a year, perhaps. He'd bring some cheap trinkets, things guests left behind.' He shook his head, remembrance twisting his features. 'I don't think he was a truly bad man. But he was weak. He didn't like being with us. I could see that, even as a small child. He always looked guilty, miserable. He kept checking his watch, the whole time he was there.' Marco sighed and drained his flute of champagne. 'The visits became less frequent, as did the times he sent money. Eventually he stopped coming altogether.'

Sierra's mouth was dry, her heart pounding strangely. Marco had never told her any of this before. She'd had no idea he'd had such a childhood; he'd suffered loss and sorrow, just as she had, albeit in a different way. 'He never said goodbye?'

Marco shook his head. 'No, he just stopped coming. My mother struggled on as best as she could.' He shrugged. 'Sicily, especially back in those days, wasn't an easy place to be a single mother. But she did her best.' His mouth firmed as his gaze became distant. 'She did her best,' he repeated, and he almost sounded as if he were trying to convince himself.

'I'm sorry,' Sierra said quietly. 'That must have been incredibly difficult.'

He shrugged and shook his head. 'It was a long time ago. I left that life behind when I was sixteen and I never looked back.'

Just like she had, except he would never understand her reasons for leaving, for needing to escape. *Not unless she told him.*

Considering all he'd just told her, Sierra felt, for the first time, that she could tell Marco the truth of her childhood. She wanted to. She opened her mouth to begin, searching for the right words, but he spoke first.

'That's why I'm so grateful to your father for giving me a chance all those years ago. For believing in me when no one else did. For treating me more like a son than my own father did.' He shook his head, his expression shadowed with grief. 'I miss him,' he said quietly, his tone utterly heartfelt.

Bile churned in her stomach and she nodded mechanically. The memories Marco spoke of were so far from her own reality of a man who had only shown her kindness in public. He'd chuck her under the chin, heft her onto his shoulders, tell the world she was his little *bellissima*. And everyone had believed it. Marco had believed it. Why shouldn't he?

And in that moment she knew she could never tell him the truth. Not when his own family life had been so sadly lacking, not when her father had provided the love and support he'd needed. She'd had her own illusions ripped away once. She wouldn't do the same to him, to anyone, and for what purpose? In three days she'd be back in London, and she and Marco need never see each other again.

CHAPTER EIGHT

BY THE TIME they were settled in the first-class compartment on the flight to New York, Sierra had restored her equilibrium. Mostly. She felt as if she were discovering a whole new side to Marco, deeper and intriguing layers, now that they'd laid aside the resentment and hostility about the past.

She was remembering how kind and thoughtful he could be, how he saw to her small comforts discreetly, how he cocked his head, his mouth quirking in a smile as he listened to her, making her feel as if he really cared what she said.

She didn't think it was an act this time. She hoped it wasn't. The truth was she still didn't trust herself. Didn't trust anyone. But the more time she spent with Marco, the more her guard began to lower.

And she was enjoying simply chatting to him over an amazingly decadent three-course meal, complete with fine crystal and china and a bottle of very good wine. She liked feeling important and interesting to him, and she was curious about his life and ambitions and interests. More curious than she'd been seven years ago, when she'd seen him as little more than a means to an end—to escape. Now she saw him as a man.

'It was your idea to bring Rocci Hotels to North America?' she asked as she spooned the last of the dark chocolate mousse they'd been served for dessert.

He hadn't said as much, but she'd guessed it from the way he'd been describing the New York project. He'd clearly been leading the charge.

'The board wasn't interested in expansion,' Marco answered with a shrug. 'They've never liked risk.'

'So it's even more important that this succeeds.'

'It will. Especially since you've agreed.' His warm gaze rested on her, and Sierra felt her insides tingle in response. It would be so easy to fall under Marco's charm again, especially since this time it felt real. But where would any of it lead? They had no future. She knew that. But she still enjoyed talking to him, being with him. She even enjoyed that tingle, dangerous as it was.

The steward dimmed the lights in the first-class cabin and Marco leaned over her seat to let it recline. Sierra sucked in a hard breath at the nearness of his body, the intoxicating heat of him. His head was close to hers as he murmured, 'You should get rest while you can. Tomorrow will be a big day.'

She nodded wordlessly, her gaze fastened on his, and gently Marco tucked a strand of hair behind her ear. It was the merest of touches, it meant nothing, and yet still she felt as if he'd given her an electric shock, her whole body jolting with longing. Marco smiled and then settled back in his own seat, stretching his long legs out in front of him as his seat dipped back. 'Get some sleep if you can, Sierra.'

Marco shifted in his seat, trying to get comfortable. It was damned difficult when desire was pulsing in his centre, throbbing through his veins. It had been nearly impossible to resist touching Sierra as they'd talked. And he'd enjoyed the conversation, the sharing of ideas, the light banter. He'd even been glad, in a surprising way, to have told her more about his past. He hadn't been planning to reveal the deprivations of his childhood and he'd kept some of it back, not wanting to invite her pity. But to see her face softened in sympathy…to know that she cared about him, even in that small way, affected him more than he was entirely comfortable with.

He'd been glad to move on to lighter topics, and Sierra had thankfully taken his cue. He'd enjoyed talking with her seven years ago, but she'd been a girl then, innocent and unsophisticated. The years had sharpened her, made her stronger and more interesting. And definitely more desirable.

In the end he hadn't been able to resist. A small caress, his fingers barely grazing her cheek as he'd tucked her hair behind her ear. He could tell Sierra was affected by it, though, and so was he. He longed to take her in his arms, even here in the semiprivacy of their seats, and plunder her mouth and body. Lose himself in her sweetness and feel her tremble and writhe with pleasure.

Stifling a groan, Marco shifted again. He needed to stop thinking like this. Stop remembering what Sierra's naked body had looked like as she'd been splayed across the piano bench, her skin golden and perfect in the lamplight. Stop remembering how silky she'd felt, how delicious she'd tasted, how overwhelming her response to him had been.

Marco clenched his eyes shut as a sheen of sweat broke out on his forehead. Next to him Sierra shifted and sighed, and the breathy sound made another spasm of longing stab through him. It was going to be a long flight. Hell, it was going to be a long three days. Because one thing he knew was he wouldn't take advantage of Sierra again.

He must have fallen into a doze eventually, because he woke to find her sitting up and smiling at him. Her hair was in delightful disarray about her face and she gave him a playful look as he straightened.

'You snore, you know.'

He drew back, caught between affront and amusement. 'I do not.'

'Hasn't anyone ever told you before?'

'No, because I don't snore.' And because he'd never had a woman stay the night to tell him so. Since Sierra, his love life—if he could even call it that—had been comprised of one-night stands and week-long flings. He'd had no intention of being caught again.

'Not very loudly,' Sierra informed him with an impish smile. 'And not all the time. But you do snore. Trust me.'

Trust me. The words seemed to reverberate through him before Marco shook them off. 'I suppose I'll have to take your word for it. And I might as well tell you that *you* drool when you sleep.'

'Oh!' Mortification brightened her cheeks as one hand clapped to her mouth. Marco instantly regretted his thoughtless quip. He'd been teasing and it wasn't true anyway; she'd looked adorable when she slept, her chin tucked towards her chest, her golden lashes fanning across her cheeks.

'Actually, you don't,' he said gruffly. 'But I couldn't say you snored, since you don't.'

'You cad.' Laughing, she dropped her hand to hit him lightly on the shoulder, and before he thought through what he was doing he wrapped her hand in his, savouring the feel of her slender fingers enclosed in his, the softness of her skin. Her eyes widened and her breath shortened.

Always it came back to this. The intense attraction that seemed only to grow stronger with every minute they spent in each other's company. Carefully, Marco released her hand. 'We'll be landing soon.'

Sierra nodded wordlessly, cradling her hand as if it was tender, almost as if he'd hurt her with his touch.

The next few hours were taken up with clearing Customs and then getting out of the airport. Marco had arranged for a limo to pick them up but nothing could be done about the bumper-to-bumper traffic they encountered all the way into Manhattan.

Finally the limo pulled up in front of The Rocci New York, a gleaming, needle-like skyscraper that overlooked Central Park West.

'It's gorgeous,' Sierra breathed as she stepped out of the limo and tilted her head up to the sky. 'I feel dizzy.'

'I hope you're not scared of heights.' He couldn't resist putting his hand on the small of her back as he guided her towards the marble steps that led up to the hotel's entrance. 'We're staying on the top floor.'

'Are we?' Her eyes rounded like a child's with excitement and Marco felt a deep primal satisfaction at making her happy. This was what he'd wanted seven years ago: to show the world to Sierra, to give it to her. To see her smile and know he'd been the one to put it there. No, he hadn't loved her, but damn it, he'd *liked* her. He still did.

'Come on,' he urged as they mounted the steps. He realised he was as excited as she was to see the hotel, to share it with her. 'Let me show The Rocci New York.'

Sierra followed Marco into the hotel's soaring foyer of marble and granite, everything sleek and modern, so unlike the faded old world elegance of the European Rocci hotels. This was something new and different, something created solely by Marco, and Sierra liked it all the more for that reason. There were no hard memories to face here, just anticipation for all that lay ahead.

Marco spoke to someone at the concierge desk while

Sierra strolled around the foyer, admiring the contemporary art that graced the walls, the sleek leather sofas and chairs and tables of polished wood. Everything felt clean and polished, sophisticated and streamlined. Empty, too, as the first guests would not arrive until tomorrow, after the official opening. Tomorrow night the hotel would have a gala in its ballroom to celebrate, and then the next day she'd fly back to London. But she'd enjoy every moment of being here.

Marco returned to her side, a key card resting in his palm. 'Ready?'

'Yes…' She eyed the key card uncertainly. 'Are we staying in the same room?'

The smile he gave her was teasingly wolfish. 'Don't worry, there's plenty of room for two.'

It didn't feel like there was plenty of room, Sierra thought as she stepped into the mirrored lift that soared straight towards the sky. The lift was enormous, their hotel suite undoubtedly far larger, and yet she felt the enclosed space keenly; Marco's sleeve brushed her arm as he stood next to her and Sierra's pulse jerked and leapt in response.

She needed to get a handle on her attraction. Either ignore it or act on it. And while the latter was a thrilling possibility, the former was the far wiser thing to do. She and Marco had way too much complicated history to think about getting involved now, even if just for a fling.

But what a fling it would be…

She could hardly credit she was thinking this way, and about *Marco*. What had happened to the man who had seemed so cold, so hostile? And what about the man she'd fled from seven years ago, whom she'd felt she couldn't trust? Had it all really changed, simply because he'd finally been honest? Or had *she* changed and let go of the past, at least a little? Enough to make her contemplate an affair.

Not, she reminded herself, that Marco was thinking along the same lines. But she didn't think she was imagining the tension that coiled and snapped between them. It wasn't merely one-sided. She hoped.

The lift doors opened into the centre of the suite and Marco stepped aside so she could walk out first.

'Welcome to the penthouse.'

Sierra didn't speak for a moment, just absorbed the impact of her surroundings. The penthouse suite was circular, with floor-to-ceiling windows surrounding her so she felt as if she were poised above the city, ready to fly.

Marco's footsteps clicked across the smooth floor of black marble as he switched on some lights. 'Do you like it?' he asked, and he almost sounded uncertain.

'Like it?' Sierra turned in a circle slowly, taking everything in: the luxurious but understated furnishings, nothing taking away from the spectacular panoramic view of the city. 'I love it. It's the most amazing room I've ever seen.' She turned to him, gratified and even touched to see the relief that flashed across his face before he schooled his features into a more neutral, composed expression. 'But surely this isn't the whole suite?' The circular room was a living area only. 'I don't see any beds. Or a bathroom, for that matter.'

'The rest of the suite is upstairs. But I wanted to show you this first.'

'It really is amazing. You must have a fantastic architect.'

'I do, but the idea for this suite was mine.' Sierra saw a slight blush colour Marco's high cheekbones and she felt an answering wave of something almost like tenderness. 'He didn't think it was possible, and I nagged him until he conceded it was.'

'Clearly you're tenacious.'

'When I have to be.'

His gaze held hers for a moment and she wondered at the subtext. Was he talking about them? If she'd confessed her fears to him all those years ago, would he have been tenacious in helping to assuage them, in making their marriage work? It was so dangerous to think that way, and yet impossible to keep herself from wondering. But she didn't want to imagine what life could have been; she wanted to think about what still could be.

'Let me show you the upstairs,' Marco said and took her hand as he led her to the spiral staircase in the centre of the room, next to the lift, that led to the rooms above.

Upstairs there were still the soaring views, although the space was divided into several rooms and the windows didn't go from ceiling to floor. Marco showed her the kitchen, the two sumptuous bedrooms with luxurious en suite bathrooms, and Sierra noted the small amount of hallway between them. There was room for two as Marco had assured her, but they would be sleeping right across from each other. The prospect filled her with excitement and even anticipation rather than alarm.

What was happening to her?

'You should refresh yourself,' Marco said when he'd shown her the guest room that she would use. 'Rest if you need to. It's been a long day.'

'Okay.'

'The ribbon-cutting and gala are tomorrow but if you feel up for it we could see a few sights today,' Marco suggested. 'If you're up for it?'

'Definitely. Let me just get changed.'

As she showered and dressed, Sierra gave herself a mental talking-to. She was playing a dangerous game, she knew, and one she hadn't intended to play. She was attracted to Marco and she was discovering all over again how much she liked him. She knew he was attracted to her; maybe he even liked her. They had plenty of reasons to have a nice time together, even to have a fling.

It didn't have to be for ever. They'd contemplated marriage once before, a marriage based on expediency rather than love, but they didn't have to this time. This time whatever was between them could be for pleasure. In her mind it sounded simple and yet Sierra knew the dangers. Trusting any man, even with just her body, was a big step, and one she hadn't taken before. Did she really want to with Marco?

And yet the three days that stretched so enticingly in front of her, the excitement of being with Marco... How could she resist?

But perhaps she wouldn't need to. Perhaps Marco had no intention of acting on the attraction between them. Perhaps he'd meant what he'd said back at the villa about never touching her again.

With her thoughts still in a hopeless snarl, Sierra left her bedroom in search of Marco. She found him downstairs in the circular salon, talking in clipped English on his phone. Sierra had become fluent in English since moving to London and she could tell he was checking on the hotel's readiness for tomorrow.

'Everything okay?' she asked as Marco slid the phone into his pocket.

'Yes. Just checking on a few last-minute details. I don't want anything to go wrong, not even the hors d'oeuvres.'

He smiled ruefully and Sierra laid a hand on his sleeve. 'This is really important to you.'

He gazed down at her, his wry smile replaced by a sombre look. 'I told you the truth before, Sierra. The whole truth. The hotel is everything to me.'

Everything. Sierra didn't know whether to feel rebuked or relieved. She decided to feel neither, to simply enjoy the possibilities of the day. 'So what sights are you going to show me? You must have been to New York loads of times, overseeing the hotel.'

'Do you have anything you want to see in particular?'

'Whatever your favourite thing is.' She wanted to get to know this man more.

A smile curled Marco's mouth, drawing Sierra's attention to his firm and yet lush lips. Lips she still remembered the taste of, and craved. 'All right, then. Let's go.'

It wasn't until they were out on Central Park West and Marco had hailed one of the city's trademark yellow cabs that Sierra asked where they were going.

He ushered her into the cab first, sliding in next to her so their thighs were pressed together. 'The Museum of Modern Art.'

'Art!' She shook her head slowly. 'I never knew you liked art.'

'Modern art. And there are a lot of things you don't know about me.'

'Yes,' Sierra answered as Marco held her gaze, a small smile curving his wonderful mouth. 'I'm coming to realise that.'

CHAPTER NINE

MARCO COULD NOT remember a time when he'd enjoyed himself more. He and Sierra wandered around the airy galleries of the MoMA and, at some point while looking at the vast canvases and modern sculpture, he took her hand.

It felt so natural that he didn't even think about it first, just slid his hand into hers and let their fingers entwine. She didn't resist, and they spent the rest of the afternoon remarking on and joking about Klimt's use of colour and Picasso's intriguing angular forms.

'I'm not an expert, by any means,' Marco told her when they wandered out into the sunshine again. It was August and New York simmered under a summer sun, heat radiating from the pavement. 'I just like the possibility in modern art. That people dared to do things differently, to see the world another way.'

'Yes, I can understand that.' She slid him a look of smiling compassion. 'Especially considering your background.'

Marco tensed instinctively but Sierra was still holding his hand, and he forced himself to relax. She knew more about him than anyone else did, even Arturo, who had been as good as a father. Arturo had known about his background a little; he'd raised him up from being a bell-boy and, in any case, Marco knew his accent gave him away as a Sicilian street rat. But Arturo had never known about his father. He'd never asked.

'Where to now?' Sierra asked and Marco shrugged.

'Wherever you like. Are you getting tired?'

'No. I don't know how anyone can get tired here. There's so much energy and excitement. I'm not sure I'll ever get to sleep tonight.' Her innocent words held no innuendo but Marco felt the hard kick of desire anyway. She looked so lovely and fresh, wearing a floaty summery dress with her hair caught in a loose plait, her face flushed and her eyes bright. He wanted to draw her towards him and kiss her, but he resisted.

That wasn't the purpose of this trip…except now maybe it was. At least, why shouldn't it be? If they were both feeling it?

'I'd love to walk through Central Park,' Sierra said and Marco forced his thoughts back to the conversation at hand.

'Then let's do it.'

They walked uptown to the Grand Army Plaza, buying ice creams to cool off as they strolled along the esplanade. Sierra stopped in front of a young busker by the Central Park Zoo, playing a lovely rendition of a Mozart concerto. She fumbled in her pockets to give him some money and Marco stopped her, taking a bill from his wallet instead.

'Thank you,' she murmured as they continued walking.

'Why do you only play in private?' Marco asked. He was curious to know more about her, to understand the enigma she'd been to him for so long.

Sierra pursed her lips, reflecting. 'Because I did it for me. It was a way to…to escape, really. And I didn't want anyone to ruin it for me, to stop me.'

'Escape? What were you escaping from?'

Her gaze slid away from his and she licked a drip of ice cream from her thumb. 'Oh, you know. The usual.'

Marco could tell she didn't want to talk about it, and yet he found he wanted to know. Badly. He'd painted a rosy, perfect picture of her childhood; considering his own, how could he have not? She had two parents who adored her, a beautiful home, everything she could possibly want. He'd wanted to be part of that world, wanted to inhabit it with her. But now he wondered if his view of it had been a little too perfect.

'But now that you're an adult? You still play in private?'

She nodded. 'I've never wanted to be a performer. I like teaching, but I play the violin for me.' She spoke firmly and he wondered if she would ever play for him. He thought that if she did it would mean something—to both of them.

And did he want it to mean something? Did he want to become emotionally close to Sierra, never mind what happened between them physically?

It was a question he didn't feel like answering or examining, not on a beautiful summer's day with the park stretched out before them, and everything feeling like a promise about to be made. He took Sierra's hand again and they walked up towards the Fountain of Bethesda, the still waters of the lake beyond shimmering under the sun.

By early evening Marco could tell Sierra was starting to flag. He was, too, and although he wanted to spend the entire day with Sierra, he knew there was pressing business to attend to before tomorrow's opening. He took a call as they entered the hotel, flashing a quick apologetic smile at Sierra. She smiled back, understanding, and disappeared into her room in the penthouse suite while Marco stretched out on a sofa and dealt with a variety of issues related to the opening.

He loosened his collar and leaned his head back against the sofa as one of his staff droned on about the guest list for tomorrow night's gala. From upstairs he could hear Sierra moving around and then the sound of a shower being turned on. He pictured her in the luxurious glass cubicle, big enough for two, water streaming down her golden body, and his whole body tightened in desperate arousal.

'Mr Ferranti?' The woman on the other end of the line must have been speaking for a while and Marco hadn't heard a word.

'I'm sorry. Can you say that again?'

A short while later Sierra came downstairs, dressed in a T-shirt and snug yoga pants, her hair falling in damp tendrils around her face.

Marco took one look at her and ended his call. His mouth dried and his heart turned over in his chest. She was utterly delectable, and not just because of her beauty. He liked having her in his space, looking relaxed and comfortable, being part of his world. He liked it a lot.

'You've finished your calls?' she asked as she came towards him. She curled up on the other end of the long leather sofa, tucking her feet underneath her.

'For the moment. There are a lot of details to sort out but first I think I want to eat.' His eyes roved over her hungrily and a blush touched her cheeks. Marco smiled and gestured to the city lights sparkling in every direction. 'The world is our oyster. What would you like to eat? We can order takeaway. Whatever you want.'

'How about proper American food? Cheeseburgers and French fries?'

He laughed and pressed a few buttons on his phone. 'And here I thought you'd be asking for lobster and caviar and champagne. Consider it done.'

* * *

Sierra watched as Marco put in their order for food. She felt jet-lagged and sleepy and relaxed, and she laid her head back against the sofa as Marco tossed his phone on the table and rose in one fluid movement.

'I'm going to get changed. The food should be here in a few minutes.'

'Okay.' It felt incredibly pleasant, no, wonderful, to sit there and listen to him go upstairs. The snick of a door closing, and she could imagine his long, lean fingers unbuttoning his shirt, shrugging it off his broad shoulders. He was the most beautiful man she'd ever seen. She remembered the feel of his body against hers, her breasts crushed against his chest…

A smile curved Sierra's mouth and she closed her eyes, picturing the scene perfectly. Then she imagined going up those stairs herself, opening that door. What would she say? What would she do? Perhaps she wouldn't have to do or say anything. Perhaps Marco would see her and take control, draw her towards him and kiss her as she wanted him to.

'I think the food's here.'

Sierra's eyes flew open and she saw Marco standing in front of her, wearing jeans and a faded grey T-shirt that clung to his pecs. His hair was slightly mussed, his jaw shadowed with stubble, and she didn't think she'd ever seen anything as wonderful, as desirable.

'You look like you were about to drop off,' Marco remarked as he took the food from the attendant who stepped out of the lift.

'I think I was.' She wasn't about to admit what had been going through her head. The mouth-watering aroma of cheeseburgers and fries wafted through the room and Marco brought the tray of food to the coffee table in front of the sofa.

'We might as well eat here.'

He handed her a plate heaped with a huge burger and plenty of fries and Sierra bit in, closing her eyes as the flavours hit her. 'Oh, this is *good*.'

Marco made a choked sound and Sierra opened her eyes, her heart seeming to still as his hot gaze held hers. 'Look like that much longer and I'll have to forget about this meal,' he said, his voice a low growl, and awareness shivered through her.

'It's too delicious to do that,' she protested, her voice breathy, and Marco shrugged, his gaze never leaving hers.

'I can think of something more delicious.'

Colour flooded her face and heated her body. This was so dangerous, and yet…why shouldn't she? Why shouldn't *they*? They were in a glamorous hotel in one of the most amazing cities in the world. There was nothing, absolutely nothing, to keep them from acting on the desire Sierra knew they both felt.

Marco plucked one of her French fries from her plate. 'Your face is the colour of your ketchup.'

She laughed shakily and put her burger down, wiping her hands on the napkin provided. 'Marco…' She trailed off, not knowing what to say or how to say it.

Marco smiled and nodded towards her still full plate. 'Let's eat, Sierra. It's a big day tomorrow.'

That sounded and felt like a brush-off. Trying not to feel stung, Sierra started eating again. Had Marco changed his mind? Why did he say one thing and then do another? Maybe, Sierra reflected, he felt as conflicted as she did. Maybe a fling would be too complicated, considering their history.

Considering her lack of experience, she didn't even know if she could handle a fling. Would she be able to walk away after a couple of days, heart intact? The truth was, she had no idea.

Marco's phone rang before they'd finished their meal and he excused himself to take the call. Sierra ate the rest of her burger and then tidied up, leaving the tray of dirty dishes by the lift. She wandered around the living area for a bit, staring out at the glittering cityscape, before jet lag finally overcame her and she headed upstairs to bed. Marco was still closeted in his own bedroom and so, with a sigh of disappointment, Sierra went into hers. Despite her restlessness, sleep claimed her almost instantly.

When she woke the sun was bathing the city in gold and she could hear Marco moving around across the hall.

The ribbon-cutting ceremony was that afternoon, and it occurred to Sierra as she showered and dressed that she really didn't have the right clothes.

Back in London, her one smart day dress and second-hand ball gown had seemed sufficient but now that she'd been to the hotel, now that she cared about it—and Marco's success—she realised she didn't want to stand in front of the crowd looking dowdy or underdressed. She wanted to look her best, not just for Marco and the public but for herself.

She dressed in jeans and a simple summery top and headed downstairs in search of Marco. He was standing by the window, scrolling through messages on his phone and drinking coffee, but he looked up as she came down the stairs, a smile breaking across his face.

'Good morning.'

'Good morning.' Suddenly Sierra felt shy. Marco looked amazing, freshly showered, his crisp blue shirt set off by a darker blue suit and silver tie. His hair was slightly damp, curling around his ears, and his smoothly shaven jaw looked eminently touchable. Kissable.

'Did you sleep well?'

'Yes, amazingly. But I wondered if there was time to go out this morning, before the opening.'

'Go out? Where?'

'Shopping.' Sierra flushed. 'I don't think the clothes I brought are…well, nice enough, if I'm honest.' She let out an uncertain laugh. 'A second-hand ball gown from a charity shop doesn't seem appropriate, now that I'm here.'

Surprise flashed across Marco's face before it was replaced by composed determination. 'Of course. I'll arrange a car immediately.'

'I can walk…'

'Nonsense. It will be my great pleasure to buy clothes for you, Sierra.' His gaze rested on her, his silvery-grey eyes seeming to burn right through her.

'You don't have to buy them, Marco—'

'You would deny me such a pleasure?' He slid his phone into his pocket and strode towards her. 'The car will be waiting. You can have breakfast on the way.'

Within minutes Sierra was whisked from the penthouse suite to the limo waiting outside the hotel; a carafe of coffee, another of freshly squeezed orange juice and a basket of warm croissants were already set out for her.

'Good grief.' She shook her head, laughing, as Marco slid into the seat next to her. 'This is kind of crazy, you know.'

'Crazy? Why?'

'The luxury. I'm not used to it.'

'You should get used to it, then. This is the life you would have had, Sierra. The life you deserve.'

She paused, a croissant halfway to her mouth, and met his gaze. 'The life I would have had? You mean if I'd married you?' She spoke softly, hesitant to dredge up the past once again and yet needing to know. Did Marco wish things had been different? Did she?

'If you'd married anyone,' Marco said after a pause.

'Someone of your father's choosing, of your family's station.'

'You think I should have married someone of my father's choosing?'

'I think you should have married me.'

Her insides jolted so hard she felt as if she'd missed the last step in a staircase. 'Even now?' she whispered.

Marco glanced away. 'Who can say what would have happened, how things would have been? The reality is you chose not to, and we've both become different people as a result.'

But people who could find their way back to each other. The words hovered on her lips but Sierra didn't say them. What were they really talking about here? A fling, a relationship, or just what might have been? She didn't know what she felt or wanted

'Ah, here we are,' Marco said, and Sierra turned to see the limo pull up to an exclusive-looking boutique on Fifth Avenue. She stuffed the rest of her croissant into her mouth as he jumped out of the limo. She swallowed quickly and then took his hand as he led her out of the car and into the boutique.

Several assistants came towards them quickly and Sierra glanced around at the crystal chandeliers, the white velvet sofas, the marble floor. There seemed to be very few pieces of clothing on display. And she felt underdressed to go shopping, which seemed ridiculous, but she could not deny the svelte blonde assistants were making her feel dowdy.

But then Marco turned to her, his eyes lit up as his warm, approving gaze rested on her. 'And now,' he said, tugging her towards him, 'the fun begins.'

CHAPTER TEN

MARCO STRETCHED OUT on the sofa, handling business calls while Sierra tried on outfit after outfit, shyly pirouetting in front of him in each one. He couldn't think of a better way to spend his time than watch Sierra model clothes. Actually, he could. He'd like to spend his time taking the clothes off her.

She'd started with modest day outfits, but even tailored skirts and crisp blouses sent his heart rate skyrocketing. He wanted to slip those pearl buttons from their holes and part the silky fabric to see the even silkier skin beneath. He wanted to shimmy that pencil skirt off her slim hips.

Instead he issued a terse command to the fawning assistant. 'We'll take them all.'

Sierra was in the dressing room and didn't hear him; a few minutes later she came out, frowning uncertainly. 'I think maybe that blue shift dress might be the best choice…'

'You can decide later,' Marco answered indulgently. It amused him that Sierra thought he was going to be satisfied by simply buying her a single outfit. What kind of man did she think he was?

A man who was falling in love with her.

The words froze inside him, turned everything to ice. He couldn't be falling in love. He didn't *do* love. He'd seen what it had done to his mother. He'd felt what it had done to him. Waiting for someone who wasn't going to come back, who didn't feel the same way. His mother. *Sierra.* And he hadn't even loved Sierra, back then. Did he want to set himself up for an even harder fall?

No, he was not falling in love with her. He was just enjoying himself. And yes, he might be thinking about what might have been; it was damned hard not to. Seeing Sierra in her element, where she belonged, every inch the Rocci heiress, her desire shining in her eyes…how could he not think about it?

'What do you think about this one?' Sierra emerged from the dressing room in an evening gown, a blush touching her cheeks. Marco stared at her, his whole body going rigid. The dress was a long, elegant column of grey-blue silk that matched her eyes perfectly. A diamanté belt encircled her narrow waist, and her hair was loose and tousled about her shoulders.

Marco couldn't even think when he saw her in that dress. 'We'll take it.' He bit the words out gruffly, and Sierra's eyes widened.

'But if you don't like it…'

'I like it.' From the corner of his eye Marco saw an assistant smile behind her hand. 'Please go wrap up the other outfits,' he barked and she melted back into the boutique, leaving them alone.

'The other outfits?' Sierra frowned. 'But I thought you were just buying the blue dress.'

'You thought wrong.' He stalked towards her and to his satisfaction he could see a pulse begin to hammer in her throat. 'I'm buying them all, Sierra. I want to see you in them all.'

She pressed a hand to her fluttering pulse as she swal-

lowed convulsively. 'There are a few more evening gowns
to try on...'

'And I want you to try them on. But I think I'd better
help you with the zipper on that dress.'

Her eyes had gone huge, as blue and glassy as twin
mountain lakes. Her pink lips parted, and when her tongue
darted out to moisten them, Marco groaned.

'The assistant...' she murmured and he shook his head,
everything in him demanding that he touch her. Now.

'Is gone. I'll do it.' Gently but purposefully, he pushed
her back into the dressing room, drawing the thick bro-
cade curtain closed behind them. The space was private,
the silence hushed and expectant. After a second when she
just stared at him, Sierra turned and offered him her back.

Marco moved the heavy, honeyed mass of her hair, revelling in the softness of it as it slipped through his fingers.
With the nape of her neck bare he couldn't keep from kissing her. He brushed his lips against the tender skin and felt
her whole body shudder in response.

She swayed against him silently and he put his hands
on her shoulders to steady her. Desire raged through him,
a fierce and overwhelming need that obliterated all rational thought. He'd take her right in this dressing room if
she'd let him, but he didn't want their first time together
to be urgent and rushed. No, he'd take his time, prolong
the exquisite agony.

Slowly Marco drew the zip down the dress, the snick
of the fabric parting one of the most erotic sounds he'd
ever heard.

The strapless dress slipped from her body, leaving her
bare, her skin golden and perfect. He slid his hands around
her waist, spanning it easily, and then, because he couldn't
keep himself from it, he slid them up to cup her breasts,

his thumbs flicking over her nipples, his hands full of her lush softness.

Sierra sagged against him, her breath coming out in a shudder. Marco pushed into her, and she gasped again at the feel of his arousal against her bottom.

When she pushed back gently, her hips nudging him with intent, he almost abandoned his resolution to take his time. It would be so easy, so overwhelmingly satisfying, to pull her dress up and bury himself inside her right then and there.

He slid his hands back down to her hips, anchoring her against him, pushing into her and having her push back, their bodies moving in an ancient rhythm. Sierra's breath caught on a gasp and her whole body went tense. Marco knew she was close to climaxing, just from this. Hell, so was he.

'Mr Ferranti?' The musical trill of the assistant's voice caused reality to rush in. Sierra stiffened and reluctantly Marco eased back.

'We're not finished here,' he told her in a low voice.

Sierra let out a laugh that sounded close to a sob. 'Dear heaven, I hope not.'

He smiled as he kissed the nape of her neck once more and then slipped from the dressing room to deal with the ill-timed assistant.

As soon as Marco had gone Sierra sank onto one of the padded benches, the dress pooling around her waist, her head in her hands. Her whole body trembled with the aftershocks of his touch. She'd been so close to losing control, and simply by the feel of his body pressing into hers. And as amazed and mortified as she felt that she'd been so shameless in a public dressing room, the overwhelming feeling she had now was a desire to rush out of this shop, jump in a limo and race back to the hotel where Marco could make good on his promise.

We're not finished.

Not, Sierra hoped, by a long shot.

'Sierra?' Marco called, his voice sounding crisply professional and not as if he were remotely affected by what had just happened between them. 'We should be getting on. You'll need to leave some time to get ready and I have a few things to finish before the opening.'

'Of course.' Hurriedly, she slithered out of the evening gown. 'Let me just get dressed.' She yanked on her jeans and pulled her T-shirt over her head, finger-combing her tousled hair as she slipped from the dressing room, her body still weak and trembling from their encounter. Marco, of course, looked completely unruffled. Maybe this was a normal experience for him. 'What about the evening gown…?' she asked, glad her voice came out sounding even.

'We're taking them all,' Marco informed her blithely. 'The assistant will have them wrapped and sent to the hotel. It's all taken care of.'

'Taking *all* of the evening gowns? But I didn't even try them on.'

'I'm sure you'll look fabulous in them. And if you don't like any of them, I'll arrange for them to be returned.' Marco took her elbow. 'Now, the limo is waiting.'

Sierra let herself be ushered out of the store, amazed by the whole experience, from the sheer number of clothes Marco had bought her to the exciting interlude in the dressing room.

'You make everything seem so easy,' she commented as she slid into the limo. 'Like the world is at your fingertips, or even your feet.'

Marco gave her a quick smile as he checked his phone. 'I've worked hard to have it be so.'

'I know you have. But do you ever...do you ever feel like pinching yourself, that this is your reality?'

For a second Marco's gaze became distant, shuttered. Then he turned back to his phone. 'Money doesn't buy everything,' he said, his voice clipped. 'No matter how many people think so, it can't make you happy.'

The honest statement, delivered as it was so matter-of-factly, both surprised and moved her. 'Are you happy, Marco?'

He glanced up with a wolfish grin. 'I was very happy with you in the dressing room. And I intend to be even happier before the day is done.'

She felt a flush spread across her body as her insides tingled. She knew Marco was deliberately avoiding a serious conversation, but she wanted him too much to care. 'I hope you do mean that.'

He paused, lowering his phone. 'I do mean it, Sierra. I want you very badly. So badly I almost lost control in a dressing room, which is something I've never done before.'

'You haven't?' she teased, trying to ignore the jealousy that spiked through her. 'I imagine you've got quite a lot of experience under your belt.'

'Not as much as you probably think, but I know my way around.' Her face heated even more and she looked away. Yes, he most certainly did. 'What about you?' he asked abruptly. 'You must have had lovers over the last seven years.' She opened her mouth to admit the truth but before she could he held up a hand. 'Never mind. I don't want to know.' His face had hardened into implacable lines, and his eyes blazed. 'But make no mistake, Sierra. I want you. Tonight.'

'I want you, too,' she whispered.

His gaze swept over her, searching, assessing. 'We're not who we were seven years ago. Things are different now.'

'I know.' She lifted her chin and met his gaze directly. 'I know what this is, Marco. We're in an amazing city for a short period of time and we happen to be attracted to each other. *Very* attracted. So why shouldn't we act on it?' She smiled, raising her eyebrows, making it sound so simple. As if she had had this kind of experience before. 'It's a fling.'

'Yes,' Marco said slowly. 'That's exactly what it is.'

Back in the hotel, Marco disappeared into the office to deal with some business before the opening while Sierra headed upstairs to the penthouse. The elegant lobby was bustling with staff as they prepared for the champagne and chocolate reception that would immediately follow the opening. And then, tonight, the ball…

Staff hurried and worked around her as she walked towards the private penthouse lift. One middle-aged man caught her eye and executed a stiff bow. 'Good afternoon, Miss Rocci. I hope you find everything to your satisfaction.'

'Yes, yes, of course,' Sierra nearly stammered. She was shaken by the way the man knew her, knew she was a Rocci. She hadn't truly been a Rocci in seven years. She'd turned her back on it all, and in that moment the memories came back in a sickening rush—the hotel openings so different from the modern elegance of The Rocci New York and yet so frighteningly familiar.

'Miss Rocci? Are you all right?' The man who had spoken to her before touched her elbow cautiously and Sierra realised she must have looked unwell. She felt sick and faint, and she reached out a hand to the lift door to steady herself.

'I'm fine. Thank you. I just haven't eaten today.'

'I'll have something sent up to your room.'

'Thank you,' Sierra murmured. 'I appreciate it.'

The lift doors opened and she stepped inside, grateful for the privacy. For a few seconds she'd heard her father's voice, felt his hand pinch her in warning as they mounted the steps of one hotel or another.

Be a good girl, Sierra. Smile for everyone.

She could hear the implied threat in his voice, the promise of punishment if she didn't behave, all against the background of a crowd's expectant murmurings, the clink of crystal...

The lift doors opened and Sierra stumbled out into the penthouse's living area, the city stretching all around her, one hand clamped to her mouth. She swallowed down the bile and then hurried upstairs to the freestanding kitchen units and poured herself a glass of water. Dear heaven, she couldn't fall apart now. Not when the opening was about to start, everyone was waiting for her. Marco was depending on her.

Sierra closed her eyes, memory and regret and fear coursing through her in unrelenting waves. She didn't want to let Marco down. How much had changed in such a short time—six weeks ago she'd been hoping never to see him again.

And now...now she was hoping he'd make love to her tonight. She wanted to stand by his side at the opening and make him proud. *She was halfway to falling in love with him.*

Sierra's eyes snapped open. *What?* How could she be? She'd always avoided and disdained love, seen how her mother had prostrated herself at its altar and lost her soul. And now she was poised to fall in love with a man she still didn't entirely trust? Or maybe it was herself she didn't trust. She didn't trust herself to keep her head straight and her heart safe.

She was inexperienced when it came to romance or sex, and here she was, contemplating a fling? For a second Sierra wondered what on earth she was doing. And then she remembered the feel of Marco's hands on her, his body behind her, and a shiver of sheer longing went through her. She knew what she was doing—and she needed to do it.

And as for the opening… She glanced at the clock above the sink and saw with a lurch of alarm that the opening was in less than an hour. An hour until she had to face Marco and the crowds of people who would be watching her, knowing she was a Rocci who had fallen from grace. Her stomach clenched and she half wished she could cry off, even as she acknowledged that she would never leave Marco in the lurch, publicly humiliated and alone. It would be almost as bad as leaving him at the altar.

She took a deep breath and willed her nerves back. Lifted her chin and straightened her shoulders. *Show no fear.* She could do this.

Marco paced the foyer of the hotel as the reporters, celebrities and guests attending the opening of The Rocci New York waited outside the frosted glass doors. It was three minutes past two o'clock and Sierra was meant to be down here. He'd already sent a staff member upstairs to check on her; she'd promised to be down shortly. He'd thought of going up himself, but some sense, or perhaps just an innate sense of caution, had stopped him. What if she didn't want to see him now?

'We should start…' Antony, the head of the hotel, looked nervously at the waiting crowds.

'We can't start without a Rocci,' Marco snapped. He felt his 'less than' status as the non-Rocci CEO keenly then,

but worse, he felt it as a man. Sierra's lateness was too powerful a reminder of another time he'd been kept waiting.

Another time he'd felt the blood drain from his head and
the hope from his heart as he'd realised once again someone wasn't coming back. Wasn't coming at all.

He blinked back the memories, willed back the hurt
and fear. This was different. He and Sierra were both different now.

Then the lift doors opened and she stepped out, looking ethereally lovely in a mint-green shift dress—and very
pale. Her gaze darted round the empty foyer and then to
the front doors where the crowd gathered, waiting; she
took a deep breath and threw her shoulders back. Marco
frowned and started forward.

Sierra saw his frown and faltered and Marco caught her
hands in his; they were icy.

'Sierra, are you all right?'

'Yes…'

'You look ill.'

'Jet lag.' She didn't quite meet his gaze. 'Everything
has been such a whirlwind.'

But he knew it couldn't just be jet lag. As beautiful as
she was and always would be to him, she looked awful.
'Sierra, if you're not up for it…' he began, only to stop. She
had to be up for it. The security of the company and his
place at its head rested on having a Rocci at this opening.

And yet in that moment he knew if she said she wasn't,
he would accept her word.

'I'm fine, Marco.' She squeezed his hands lightly and
gave him what he suspected was meant to be a smile. 'Really, I am. Let's do this.'

Sierra watched as Marco scanned her face like a doctor
looking for broken bones. She knew she must look truly

awful for him to seem so worried and she tried to dredge
up some confidence and composure. It was just the memories. So many of them, crowding her in like jeering ghosts.
She wanted to drown out the babble of their voices but it
was hard. She hadn't been at an opening like this since
she was a teenager, her father's hand hard on her elbow,
his voice in her ear.

Be good, Sierra. With the awful implied *or else.*

Finally Marco nodded and let go of her hands. 'All right.
The crowd is waiting.'

'I'm sorry I'm late.' She'd been trying not to be sick.

'It's fine.' He strode towards the front doors and resolutely, holding her head high, Sierra followed.

A staff member opened the doors and Sierra stepped
out into the shimmering heat and the snap and flash of
dozens of cameras. She recoiled instinctively before she
forced herself to stop and straighten. Foolishly, perhaps,
she hadn't realised quite how big a deal the hotel opening would be, bigger than any of the ones her father
had arranged, but then she hadn't considered Marco's
ambition and drive.

Marco had stepped up to a microphone and was wel-
coming the guests and media, his voice smooth and ur-
bane, his English flawless. Sierra stood stiffly, trying to
smile, until Marco's words began to penetrate.

'I know Arturo Rocci, my mentor and greatest friend,
would be so proud to be here with us, and to see his daughter cutting the ribbon today. Arturo believed passionately
in the values that gird every Rocci hotel. He valued hard
work, excellent service and, of course, family ties.' He
glanced at Sierra, who stood frozen, her stomach churning. She hadn't expected Marco to mention her father. She
couldn't keep his words from washing over her like an acid
rain, corroding everything.

The crowd clapped and someone pressed an overlarge pair of gilded scissors into her hand. The silver satin ribbon that stretched across the steps glinted in the sunlight.

'Sierra?' Marco asked, his voice low.

Somehow she moved forward and snipped the ribbon. As it fell away the crowd cheered and then Marco took her elbow and led her inside to the cool sanctuary of the foyer.

'You don't look well.'

'I'm sorry, it must be the heat. And the jet lag.' *And the memories.* And her father's ghost, hurting her from the grave. Marco still believing the best of him, and she could hardly fault him. She hadn't said anything, hadn't thought it was necessary. And when she'd been planning never to see Marco again, it hadn't been. But now? Now, when she was thinking of something actually happening between them?

'Do you want to sit down?' Marco asked. 'Catch your breath?'

Sierra shook her head. 'I'm fine, Marco. I came here for this, and I'll see it through.' She plucked a flute of champagne from a waiter's tray. She definitely needed some liquid courage. Guests were starting to stream into the foyer, chatting and taking pictures. 'Let the party begin,' she said, and raised her glass in a determined toast.

CHAPTER ELEVEN

A FEW HOURS into the reception Sierra finally started to relax. The memories that had mocked her were starting to recede; her father's grip not, thankfully, as tight as she'd feared it was. She avoided reporters with their difficult, probing questions and chatted with various guests and staff about innocuous things: New York, London, the latest films. She was actually having a good time.

The three glasses of champagne helped, too.

'This is the most amazing thing I've ever seen,' she told a waiter as she studied the chocolate fountain with floating strawberries. He smiled politely and a firm hand touched her elbow. Even though Sierra couldn't see who it was, she felt it through her marrow. Marco.

'You're not drunk, are you?'

'Drunk? Thanks very much.' She turned around, misjudging the distance, and nearly poured her half-full flute of champagne onto his front. Marco caught her hand and liberated her glass. 'Slightly tipsy only,' she amended at his wry look. 'But this is a fun party.'

Marco drew her aside, away from the waiter and guests. 'You seemed tense earlier. Even upset. Was it something I said?' Concern drew his straight dark eyebrows together, his wonderful mouth drawn into a frowning line.

'No,' Sierra answered. 'It wasn't something you said.'

'Are you sure?'

She nodded, knowing she couldn't explain it to him here, and maybe not ever. The deeper things got with Marco, the harder it became to come clean about her past. She didn't want to hurt him, and yet if they were to have any future at all she knew she needed to explain. He needed to understand.

But why was she even thinking about a future? They were just having a fling. And they hadn't even had it yet.

'When is the ball tonight?'

'Not for a few hours. But if you'd like to retire upstairs and get ready, you can. You've shown your face here. You've done enough.' He paused, and then rested a hand on her arm. 'Thank you, Sierra.'

Marco watched Sierra head towards the lift, a frown on his face. She'd looked so pale and shaky when she'd first come to the opening, almost ill. Something was wrong and he had no idea what it was.

At least she'd rallied, smiling and talking with guests, her natural charm and friendliness coming to the fore. She'd maybe rallied a little too much, judging by the amount of champagne she'd imbibed. The thought made him smile.

He was looking forward to seeing Sierra tonight at the ball, and then after. Most definitely after.

'Mr Ferranti, do you have anything to say about Sierra Rocci's presence at the opening today?'

Marco turned to see one of the tabloid reporters smirking at him.

'No, I do not.'

'You were engaged to Sierra Rocci seven years ago, were you not?' the weedy young man pressed. 'And she broke off the engagement at the last moment? Left you standing at the altar?' He smirked again and Marco stiffened, longing to wipe that smug look off the man's face.

He hadn't considered the press resurrecting that old story. His engagement to Sierra had been kept quiet back then; Arturo had wanted a quiet ceremony, not wanting to expose Sierra to media scrutiny. Marco had been glad to agree.

'Well?' The reporter smirked, eyebrows raised.

'No comment,' Marco bit out tersely, and stalked off.

'You can look in the mirror now.'

'Thank you.' Sierra smiled at the stylist, Diana, whom Marco had arranged to do her hair and make-up for the ball. It had been a nice surprise to emerge from an hour-long soak in the sunken marble tub to find a woman ready to be her fairy godmother.

Now Sierra turned around and gazed at her reflection in the full-length mirror, catching her breath on a gasp of surprise.

'Oh, my goodness…'

'My sentiments exactly,' Diana agreed cheerfully.

Sierra raised one hand to touch the curls that were piled on top of her head, a few trailing down to rest beguilingly on her shoulder. Diamond clips sparkled from the honeyed mass and when she turned her head they caught the light. Her make-up was understated and yet somehow transformed her face; she had smoky eyes, endless lashes, sculpted cheekbones and lush pink lips.

'I had no idea make-up could do so much,' she exclaimed and leaned forward to peer at herself more closely.

Diana laughed. 'I didn't use that much make-up. Just enough to enhance what was already there.'

'Even so.' Sierra shook her head, marvelling. She had never worn make-up as a teenager, and she hadn't changed much during her years in London. Now, however, she could see the advantages.

Her gaze dropped from her face to her dress. She'd chosen the dress Marco had seen her in, the silvery-blue column of silk with the diamanté belt around her waist. Looking at herself in the dress made her face warm and her blood heat as she remembered how Marco had unzipped it. How he'd put his hands on her hips and pulled her towards him and she'd gone, craving the feel of him, desperately wanting more.

'I wonder if I put a bit too much blusher on,' Diana mused and, with a suppressed laugh, Sierra turned away from the mirror.

'I'm sure it's fine.'

Marco was getting ready just across the hall, and she couldn't wait to see him. She couldn't wait for him to see her, and for this wonderful, enchanted evening to begin. No matter what had happened before or might lie ahead, she wanted to truly be Cinderella and enjoy this one magical night. The clock wasn't going to strike just yet.

Marco knocked softly on her bedroom door and, with a conspiratorial grin, Diana went to answer it. 'I'll tell him you're coming in a moment. You're going to knock his socks off, you know.'

Sierra smiled back, one hand pressed to her middle to soothe the seething nerves that had started in her stomach. She didn't want anything to ruin this night.

Diana told Marco with surprising bossiness to wait for Sierra downstairs and, after taking the filmy matching wrap and beaded bag, Sierra opened the door and headed out.

She walked down the spiral staircase carefully; the last thing she wanted was to go flying down the stairs and fall flat on her face.

She saw Marco before he saw her; he was standing by the windows, staring out at the city where the sky was lit up with streaks of vivid orange and umber, a spectacular summer sunset.

Her heels clicked on the wrought iron and he turned around, going completely still as he caught sight of her. Sierra couldn't tell anything from his face; his perfect features were completely blank as his silvery-grey gaze swept over her.

She came to the bottom of the staircase, her heart starting to beat hard. 'Do I…? Is everything all right?'

Suddenly she wondered if she had lipstick on her teeth or she'd experienced some unknown wardrobe malfunction.

Then Marco's face cleared and he stepped forward, taking her hands in his. 'You have stolen my breath along with my words. You are magnificent, Sierra.'

A smile spread across her face as he squeezed her hands. 'You look pretty good yourself.'

Actually he looked amazing. The crisp white tuxedo shirt was the perfect foil for his olive skin, and the tailored midnight-dark tuxedo emphasised the perfect, powerful musculature of his body. Marco wasn't the only one who was breathless.

He touched her cheek with his fingertips, and the small touch seemed to Sierra like a promise of things to come. *Wonderful* things to come. 'We should go, if you're ready.'

'I am.'

The gala was in the hotel's ballroom, several floors below the penthouse yet with the same spectacular view from every side. Sierra stepped into the huge room with a soft gasp of appreciation. The room was as sleekly spare and elegant as the hotel foyer, letting the view be its main decoration. Tuxedo-clad waiters circulated with trays of champagne and hors d'oeuvres and a string quartet played softly from a dais in one corner of the room. Sierra turned to Marco, her eyes shining.

'Did you have some say in this room, too?'

'Maybe a little.' He smiled, taking her by the hand to draw her into the ball. 'Let me introduce you.'

Sierra had never particularly liked social occasions, thanks to her father's silent, menacing pressure. Even in London she'd preferred quiet gatherings to parties or bars, and yet tonight those old inhibitions fell away. It felt different now, when she was at Marco's side. When she felt safe and confident and valued.

But not loved. Never loved.

She pushed that niggling reminder to the back of her mind as Marco introduced her to various guests—stars, socialites, business types and the odd more ordinary people, and Sierra chatted with them all. Laughed and drank champagne and felt dizzy with a new, surprising elation.

After a few hours Marco pulled her away from a crowd of women she'd been chatting with, plucking the half-drunk glass of champagne from her fingertips and thrusting it at a waiter, who whisked it away.

'What is it…?' Sierra began, only to have her words fall away as Marco drew her onto the dance floor.

His gaze was hooded and intent, the colour of his eyes like molten silver as his hands slid down to her hips and he anchored her against him.

'Dance with me.'

Sierra felt as if the breath had been vacuumed from her lungs as she wordlessly nodded, placing her hands on his broad shoulders, the fabric of his tuxedo jacket crisp underneath her fingers.

The string quartet was playing a lovely, lazy melody, something you could sway to as you lost your soul. And

Sierra knew she was in danger of losing hers, of losing everything to this man. Tonight she wasn't going to worry, wasn't even going to care. She'd let herself fall and in the morning she'd think about picking up the broken pieces.

'It seems like the ball is going well,' Sierra said as they swayed to the music. 'Are you pleased?'

'Very pleased. The hotel is booked solid for the next three months. That's in part because of you.'

'A very small part,' Sierra answered. 'You're the one who put in all the hard work. I'm proud of you, Marco.' She smiled shyly. 'I know you told me how much your job meant to you, but I realised why tonight. You're good at this. You were meant for this.'

Marco didn't speak for a few seconds; a muscle flickered in his jaw and he seemed to struggle with some emotion. 'Thank you,' he said finally. 'That means a great to deal to me.'

The song ended and another one began, and neither Marco nor Sierra moved from the dance floor. She felt as if she could stay here for ever, or at least until Marco finally, thankfully took her upstairs.

'You are the most beautiful woman in the world tonight.' Marco's voice was low, his tone too sincere for her to argue with.

'As long as you think so,' Sierra murmured.

His eyes blazed for a second, thrilling her, and he pulled her even closer to him. 'Do you mean that?'

'Yes,' she said simply. After everything that had happened, everything he'd made her feel, she knew there could be no dissembling.

Marco drew a shuddering, steadying breath and eased her a little bit away from him as he smiled wryly. 'I don't want to disgrace myself here.'

She smiled, the curve of her lips coy. 'Then disgrace yourself upstairs.'

Regret flashed across his features like a streak of pain. 'We can't leave the ball yet.'

'Do you have to stay to the end?' Some of the socialites and celebrities seemed ready to party until dawn.

'No,' Marco answered firmly. 'And even if I needed to, I wouldn't. I can't last that long without touching you, Sierra. Without being inside you.'

The huskily spoken words sent a spear of pure pleasure knifing through her. 'Good.'

Marco shook his head. 'Keep looking at me like that and I really won't last.'

'How am I looking?' Sierra asked with deliberate innocence.

'Like that.' He pulled her closer again. 'Like you want to eat me.'

'Maybe I do.' A blush pinkened her cheeks but she held his heated gaze. She could hardly believe the audacity of her words, and yet she meant them. Utterly.

Marco groaned softly. 'Do you enjoy torturing me?'

'Yes,' she answered with a shameless smile. 'It's payback for the way you tortured me this morning.'

His gaze swept over her body. 'That was torture for me, as well. Sweet, sweet torture.'

She felt as if she could melt beneath the heat of his gaze. Or maybe combust. She'd felt an intense excitement spiralling up inside her from the moment Marco had taken her onto the dance floor, and it was overwhelming now. The need for him was a physical craving, so fierce and wonderful she was helpless to its demand.

Her tongue shot out and dampened her lips as she gave him a look of complete yearning. 'Marco…'

'We're going,' Marco bit out. 'Now.' His long, lean fingers encircled her wrist as he led her purposefully from the dance floor.

In any other circumstance Sierra would have baulked at being led from the ballroom like a sulky schoolgirl or a flagrant harlot. Now the need was too much to feel even a twinge of embarrassment or anger. She just wanted to get upstairs fast.

Marco muttered a few words to one of his staff standing by the door, and then they were out in the hall, the air cool on Sierra's heated cheeks. A few guests loitering there shot them speculative looks, but Marco ignored them all. He stabbed the button for the penthouse lift and Sierra held her breath until the doors opened and Marco pulled her inside.

CHAPTER TWELVE

THE LIFT DOORS had barely closed before Marco pulled Sierra to him, her breasts colliding with his chest as his mouth came down hard on hers. He couldn't have waited another moment, not even one second, to touch her, and the feel of her lips on his wasn't the water in the desert he'd thought it would be; it was a match to the flame, igniting his need all the more.

He backed her up against the wall of the lift, his mouth plundering hers as his hands fisted in her hair. Diamond-tipped pins scattered across the floor of the lift with a tinkling sound. Marco couldn't get enough of her. He moved his hands from her hair to her hips, yanking up a satiny fistful of her dress, needing to touch her skin.

He found the curve of her neck with his mouth and sucked gently, his desire knifing inside him as Sierra groaned aloud.

'You'll ruin the dress…' she gasped.

'I'll buy you another. I'll buy you a dozen, a hundred others.'

The doors pinged open and Marco stumbled backwards into the penthouse, pulling Sierra with him. She came with him, laughing and breathless, clutching his shirt as she tried to pull it away from his cummerbund.

'I need to see you,' Marco said. He tugged at the zip at

the back of her dress. 'Now.' He tugged harder at the zip and the dress slithered off her, leaving her in nothing but a scrap of lace pants. Marco inhaled sharply at the sight of her pale golden perfection, the lights from the city gleaming on her smooth skin.

She stepped out of the dress, chin lifted, smile shy, wearing nothing but lace and stiletto heels. Marco had never seen a more magnificent sight.

'This feels a bit unequal,' she said with a little uncertain laugh. 'I'm in my birthday suit and you're completely dressed.'

He spread his arms wide. 'Then maybe you should do something about it.'

'Maybe I should.' She stepped closer to him so he could breathe in the lemon scent of her hair; it had come undone from the pins he'd pulled out in the lift and lay in twists and curls about her shoulders. She pursed her lips slightly as she fumbled with the studs on his shirt; her breasts grazed his chest every time she moved.

Finally she'd managed to release the studs; she tossed them aside with a breathless laugh and then tugged his shirt out from his cummerbund and parted it, smoothing her hands along his chest. Marco closed his eyes, his breath hissing between his teeth. It amazed him how profoundly her touch affected him. He'd been with plenty of women over the years, gorgeous women with experience and expertise and plenty of confidence, but Sierra's hesitant touch reduced all those women to a pale memory.

'You're very beautiful,' she whispered, and tugged his shirt off his body before undoing the laces of his cummerbund. He wore only his trousers now, and he saw the hesitation in Sierra's face and wondered what she'd do about it. Sometimes she seemed so innocent and inexperienced he wondered how many lovers she'd actually had. But it wasn't a train of thought he enjoyed dwelling on, and so he made himself stop thinking about it. It didn't matter. The only thing that mattered was that she was with him now.

'Well?' He arched an eyebrow, his mouth curving in a salacious smile. 'I'm not naked yet.'

'I know.' She laughed again, a soft, breathy sound, and then tugged his trousers down. Marco kicked them off his feet, and followed with his shoes and socks. Now all he wore was a pair of navy silk boxers and his arousal was all too evident.

Sierra's gaze darted up to him and she licked her lips. Marco groaned. Then she reached out a hand and touched his shaft through his boxers, her fingers questing uncertainly and then wrapping more firmly around him.

Marco clenched his jaw against the almost painful wave of pleasure that crashed over him. 'Sierra…'

'Is this okay?' She jerked her hand back as if she'd hurt him and he laughed, albeit shakily.

'More than okay. What you do to me… But I need to do some things to you.' He reached for her then, because he needed her next to him. The feel of their naked bodies colliding made them both gasp aloud, her breasts against his chest, their legs tangled.

Marco kissed her deeply and she responded with all of her clumsy ardour, tangling her hands in his hair as he fitted her body more closely to his. Marco backed her towards the wall, pressing her against the sheet of glass as Sierra let out a soft laugh.

'Half the world now has a glimpse of my backside.'

'No one can see you from up here,' he promised her, 'but, if they could, it would be the most splendid view. Not,' he added in a growl as his mouth moved down her body, 'that I want anyone to see you but me.' *Ever*, he silently added, and then pushed the thought away as he turned his attention to her breasts. Her skin was pale and gleaming in the moonlight; she looked like a statue of Athena or Artemis, naked and proud.

Sierra's head came back against the glass, her hair tumbling about her shoulders, and her legs buckled as Marco lavished his attention on each breast in turn and then moved lower.

She gasped, a ragged pant, as he parted her thighs. 'Marco…'

'I want to taste you.' Was she thinking of before, in the villa, when he'd touched her like this? Then it had been confused, born of both need and anger, a twisted revenge he hadn't wanted to articulate even to himself. Now he felt nothing but this deep physical and emotional connection he needed to act on. To show her how important she was to him. 'I want to feel you come apart beneath me,' he muttered against her. 'I want you to give me everything, Sierra.' *For ever.*

Sierra sagged against the window, Marco supporting her with one arm, as he plundered her centre. She didn't know how she could have, but she'd forgotten how intense and exquisite and *intimate* this was. Marco's hands were cupping her bottom as pleasure spiralled inside her, up and up, tighter and tighter until she felt as if she were apart from her body even as she dwelt so intensely in it. When she came, she cried out, Marco holding her to him as she slid into boneless pleasure.

A few moments passed while he cradled her and her breathing slowed and then he scooped her up in his arms and took her up the spiral staircase to his bed.

He deposited her on the navy silk sheets tenderly, like a treasure, and Sierra lay there, gazing up at him with pleasure-dazed eyes as he stripped the boxers from his body and then stretched out next to her.

Completely naked, he was magnificent, every muscle perfectly sculpted, the hard ridge of his abdomen begging for her touch. She slid her hand down his toned stomach, a thrill of wonder and pleasure shooting through her at Marco's ragged gasp. It amazed her that she affected him so much. That she had that much power. It was a heady feeling but a serious one, too, because she knew all about the abuse of power.

'You're amazing,' she whispered, and wrapped her fingers around his shaft. His skin was smooth and hot, and it thrilled her.

'*You're* amazing,' he muttered and pulled her to him, sliding a hand between her thighs, where she was still damp from his touch. 'I want you now, Sierra. I want to be inside you.'

'I want you inside me.'

He rolled on top of her, poised at her entrance as a frown furrowed his forehead. 'Birth control…'

She blushed even as she opened herself to him. 'I don't… That is, I'm not on anything.'

In one swift movement Marco rolled off her. Sierra felt the loss of him keenly. 'Marco…'

'I'm sorry. I should have thought of it sooner. I was so wrapped up in you…'

Disappointment made her feel as if she'd swallowed a stone. 'But don't you have anything?'

He arched an eyebrow, a wry smile twisting his lips. 'I wasn't expecting to need *anything* on this trip.'

'You didn't think you'd get lucky?' she teased and his expression turned serious.

'I didn't dare hope, Sierra.'

'Even so…'

'I'm not quite,' he said, 'the super stud you seem to think I am. But thanks, anyway.'

She laughed softly. 'But you must have had plenty of women…' Even if she felt like scratching their eyes out just then.

Marco's expression closed and he shook his head. 'Let's not talk about that. The past is in the past, for both of us.'

She nodded and Marco left the room. He came back seconds later, condom in hand. 'Fortunately, the penthouse is admirably stocked. Now, where were we?'

She arched her body against the sheets, eyebrows raised as a provocative smile curved her mouth. 'Right about here?'

His gaze darkened with desire as he watched her move. 'Yes, I think so. But I'd better check.'

He rolled on the condom and Sierra watched, transfixed by the sight, by the sheer beauty of him. Now would probably be a good time to tell him that she hadn't actually done any of this before. The feel of him in her hand had caused her a twinge of alarm, wondering how he was going to fit inside her. Wondering how the mechanics of this actually worked.

But she didn't want to break the moment, and she knew any explanation she gave would be clumsy and awkward. Marco had said the past was in the past. Better to leave it there.

He lay down next to her again, stirring up the embers of need into roaring flame with just a few touches, his mouth on hers, his hand between her thighs. She arched against him, a sound like a kitten's mewl emerging from her lips.

He laughed softly and then rolled on top of her, braced on his forearms as he nudged at her entrance. 'Are you ready…?'

'Yes,' she panted. *'Yes.'*

He moved inside her and Sierra stiffened instinctively at the entirely unexpected feeling. Her gaze widened and her mouth parted on a soundless gasp. She felt so…full. Invaded, yet in an exciting way. He moved again and she let out a little gasp as the first twinge of discomfort assaulted her.

Marco froze, his face twisted in a grimace of shock and restraint. 'Sierra…'

'I'm all right,' she assured him. 'Just…give me a moment.'

He stared at her in disbelief as she adjusted to the feel of him, her body expanding naturally to accommodate his. The twinges of discomfort receded and she arched upwards to take him more fully into herself. 'You can move,' she whispered. 'Slowly.'

He slid deeper inside and she gasped again, the sensation acute and overwhelming. He froze, and she let out a shaky laugh. 'This isn't quite…'

He touched his forehead to hers, his biceps bulging with the effort of holding himself back. 'Why didn't you tell me?'

'I don't know,' she confessed. 'I didn't want to ruin anything. It seemed so…' She laughed again, softly. 'I don't know.' Maybe part of her had liked the idea of Marco thinking she was experienced, worldly. Maybe part of her had wanted to match him for sophistication and expertise, even though she knew she never could. In some unvoiced corner of her heart she'd wanted to make their positions more equal.

'Are you okay?' he whispered, and she nodded. It hurt more than she'd expected, but within the hurt were flickers of pleasure, and her body arced towards those, seeking them out of instinct. Marco moved again, sliding deeper inside and then out again and Sierra tried to relax. He was so big, and he filled her so completely. It was overwhelming, both emotionally and physically, to be completely *conquered* by another person. She felt him in every nerve, every cell of her body. There was no part of her that he did not possess, and it was a complex and frightening feeling.

'Okay?' he asked again and she laughed, a hiss of sound, as she clutched his shoulders.

'Stop asking me that.'

'I don't want to hurt you.'

'You're not.' Except he was, and in a way she hadn't expected. The physical pain was nothing compared to the emotional onslaught, the sense that Marco Ferranti was battering every defence she had, leaving her completely bare. Exposed and vulnerable and *wanting*.

And even as these feelings crashed over her, pleasure came, too. Tiny at first, little whispers that promised something greater, and her body responded instinctively, arching up towards his as she wrapped her legs around his waist and drew him completely into herself. She could feel him everywhere, and it made tears start in her eyes.

Marco was moving faster now and Sierra found his rhythm and matched it, awkwardly at first and then with more grace as the sensations whirling inside her coalesced and drove her body onwards. The pain had receded and pleasure took its place, so she clutched him and threw her head back, letting out a ragged cry as she climaxed, the feeling more intense than anything she had ever experienced. Marco shuddered on top of her, his body sagging against hers even as he bore his weight on his arms.

He kissed her temple, his lips lingering against her skin. 'That was incredible.'

'Was it?' she asked, her voice trembling a little with everything she felt.

'You have to ask?' He smiled tenderly and smoothed the hair away from her flushed face.

'Well, I don't have much experience of this kind of thing. As you know.' She let out a shaky laugh and averted her face. She was, quite suddenly and inexplicably, near tears and she didn't want Marco to see.

'Sierra...' He trailed his fingers down her cheek, the gesture so tender it brought a lump to her throat. In a few seconds she'd be bawling. 'You should have told me.'

'It didn't feel like the right moment.'

'I'm not sure when a better moment would have been,' he said wryly, and then pulled out of her, rolling away to dispose of the condom. Sierra took the reprieve from his scrutiny to tidy her hair and wipe quickly at her eyes, wrapping the duvet around herself.

Marco glanced back at her, eyes narrowed. Was she so obvious? Could he see the torment and confusion in her eyes, her face? 'Are you sure you're okay?' he asked, and she nodded. 'You don't...you don't regret this?'

'No,' she whispered, because that much was true. Mostly.

He stretched out next to her, unabashedly naked, and tucked a few stray tendrils of hair behind her ear as he studied her face. 'Then why do you look like you're about to cry?'

'Because it's so *much*.' The words burst from her and a few rogue tears trickled down her cheeks. She batted at them impatiently. 'I wasn't expecting to feel so much. And I don't mean physically,' she clarified quickly. 'I'm not talking about the pleasure.'

'I hope you felt that, too.'

'You know I did,' she said, and she sounded almost cross.

Marco frowned, shaking his head. 'Then what?'

Did he not get it? But then maybe Marco hadn't felt the

emotional tidal wave that had pulled her under. Maybe she was the only one who felt so exposed, so vulnerable and needy. She felt as if Marco had stripped away everything she'd had to protect herself and left her reeling, wondering how to recover. Wondering how she would ever live without him even as terror clutched her at the thought of living with him. At being this vulnerable again, ever.

'I need to use the bathroom,' she muttered and wriggled away from him, the duvet snagging about her body.

Marco reached for her arm. 'Sierra—'

'Please, Marco.' She finally freed herself from the bed-covers and hurried towards the en suite bathroom. 'Please just let me be.'

Marco watched Sierra barricade herself in the bathroom, a frown deepening on his face. What the hell had happened? He'd had the most incredible sexual experience of his life, and he'd reduced his lover almost to tears. It didn't make sense. He knew, despite the initial pain, she'd enjoyed herself. He'd felt her climax reverberate through his own body. And he knew she'd been touched emotionally, too, but then so had he. Sex had never felt so important as it did right then.

But Sierra seemed to think that was a bad thing. She'd been tearful, cross, even angry—and why? Because she didn't want to feel those things? She didn't want to have that kind of connection with him?

The answer seemed all too obvious. Swearing under his breath, Marco rose from the bed and reached for his boxers. The intimacy they'd wrapped themselves in moments before was already unspooling, loose threads they might never knit back together, which was just as well. This was a fling, nothing more. No matter what he'd felt moments before.

And yet it still stung that Sierra was withdrawing from him. The possibility that she might regret what had happened filled him with a bitter fury he remembered too well. This time he'd be the one to walk away first. He'd make sure of it.

CHAPTER THIRTEEN

BY THE TIME Sierra emerged from the bathroom twenty minutes later she'd managed to restore her composure. Cloak herself in numbness, just like she used to during her father's rages. Strange that she was using the same coping mechanisms now, after the most intimate and frankly wonderful experience of her life, as she had then.

She unlocked the door to the bathroom and stepped out, thankfully swathed in an enormous terry-cloth dressing gown. Marco was sitting in bed, his back propped against the pillows, his legs stretched out in front of him, his arms folded. His face was unsmiling.

'Better?'

'Yes.' She tucked her hair behind her ears and came gingerly towards the bed. What was the fling protocol now? Should she thank him for a lovely time and beat it to her own bedroom? That was what she wanted to do. She wanted an out, even if the prospect filled her with an almost unbearable loneliness.

Marco arched an eyebrow. 'You're not actually thinking of leaving my bed, are you?'

It disconcerted her that he could guess her thought processes so easily. 'I thought… I thought maybe it was best.'

'Best? How so?' There was a dangerous silky tone to Marco's voice that she remembered from when she'd first seen him at the lawyer's office, and then at the villa. It made alarm prickle along her spine and she took an instinctive step backwards.

'You no doubt want your space, as do I. We know what this is, Marco.'

'What is it?'

'A fling.' She forced herself to say the words, to state it plainly. 'We're agreed on that. Nothing's changed.' Even if she felt as if her whole world had shattered when Marco had made love to her.

Love... How had she not realised how dangerous this would be? How had she not seen how much a so-called fling would affect her?

'And does having a fling mean we can't sleep together?' Marco bit out. 'Does it mean you've got to hightail it from my bed as if you've been scalded?'

Sierra stared at him in surprise, understanding trickling through her. He was *hurt*. He'd taken her sprint to the bathroom as a personal slight. The realisation softened her, evened out the balance of power she'd felt so keenly had been in his favour.

'Maybe you ought to tell me what the rules are. Since I've obviously never been in this situation before.'

'I haven't either, Sierra.' Marco rubbed a hand across his jaw as he gazed at her starkly. 'No other woman has made me feel the way you do.'

Sierra swallowed hard, a thousand feelings swarming her stomach like butterflies. Disbelief. Fear. Hope. Joy. 'Marco...'

'Don't,' he said roughly. 'Like you said, we both know what this is. But you can still stay the night.'

'Is that what you want?'

He hesitated, his jaw tight. 'Yes,' he finally bit out. 'It is.'

'It's what I want, too,' Sierra said softly.

'Good.' Marco held out his arms and she went to him easily. Suddenly it seemed like the simplest thing in the world to accept Marco's embrace. Moments ago she'd wanted to escape, but now she felt there was no other place to be.

Sierra closed her eyes and snuggled against him, wondering how a supposed fling could be so confusing and make her feel so much.

Marco woke slowly, blinking in the sunlight that streamed through the huge windows. Sierra lay curled up in his arms, her cheek resting against his bare chest. They'd slept in each other's arms all night, and Marco had marvelled at how good it had felt, how much he didn't want to move. Even if he should. No matter what he'd said last night, this felt like more than a fling…to him.

Now he eased slowly from Sierra's sleepy embrace and stole downstairs to the living area; dawn was streaking across the city sky and the first rays of sunlight were touching the skyscrapers of midtown in gold.

He gazed out of the window at the beautiful summer morning, but his thoughts were with the woman he'd left upstairs in bed. Sierra was supposed to fly back to England this afternoon. He'd booked her ticket himself. A few weeks ago it hadn't seemed an issue. He'd convinced himself that he wanted her only to open the hotel, not in his bed. In his life. *Maybe even in his heart.*

Marco let out a shuddering breath and pressed his fists to his eyes. He couldn't be in love with Sierra. He'd written off that useless emotion. He'd seen how people who supposedly loved you were able to walk away. His father. His mother. And even Sierra, seven years ago, although at least no love had been involved then. No, then it had only been a lifetime commitment. And if Sierra had been able to walk away from him then, how much more easily could she do it now?

He should let her go. Kiss her goodbye, thank her for the memories and watch her walk onto the plane and out of his life. That would be the sensible thing. It also made him recoil with instinctive, overwhelming revulsion. He didn't want to do that. He wasn't going to do that.

So what was he going to do?

Marco turned away from the window and reached for his laptop. He'd leave the question of Sierra for a little while, at least until she woke up and he got a read on what she was feeling.

He clicked on his home news page, freezing when he saw one of the celebrity headlines: *A Rocci Reunion?*

Quickly, he scanned the article, which covered the hotel opening yesterday. Very little was about the hotel; the journalist was far more interested in lurid speculation about the relationship between him and Sierra. There was even a blurry photo of him and Sierra slow-dancing last night, which infuriated him because no paparazzi had been invited to the private ball. It looked, he decided, like a snap someone had taken on their phone and then no doubt sold to the press.

Marco swore aloud.

'Marco?'

He turned to see Sierra standing in the doorway, an uncertain look on her face. She was wearing that ridiculously huge dressing gown, her hair about her shoulders in tousled golden-brown waves. She looked delectable and yet also nervous.

'Is something wrong?' she asked, and she took a step towards him.

Marco glanced back at his laptop. 'Not exactly,' he hedged. He realised he had no idea what Sierra's reaction to the news article would be. He didn't even know what *his* was. Irritation that someone had so invaded his—their— privacy. And anger that someone was plundering their shared past for a sordid news story. And, underneath all that, Marco realised, he felt fear. Shameful, hateful fear, that Sierra would see this article and be the one to walk away first.

'What does "not exactly" mean, Marco?' Sierra's gaze flicked to his laptop and then back to his face. He'd closed the browser window, thankfully, so she hadn't seen the article. But he knew he couldn't, in all good conscience, keep it from her.

'We've made the news,' he said after a pause. 'Someone must have snapped a photo of us on their phone.'

'On their phone? But why?'

'To sell to a celebrity tabloid.'

'A celebrity tabloid…' She shook her head, bewilderment creasing her forehead. 'But why would a celebrity tabloid want photos of us? I mean…I know I opened the hotel, but it's not as if I'm actually famous.' Her gaze widened. 'Are *you* famous? I mean, that famous?'

'We're famous,' Marco stated flatly. 'Together. Because of our past.'

'You mean…'

'Yes. That's exactly what I mean.' He bit out each word, realising he was sounding angry, but he couldn't keep himself from it. This was the last thing he wanted to have happen now.

'What does it say?'

After a moment's hesitation, Marco clicked to enlarge the browser window. 'See for yourself.'

Sierra stepped forward, her mouth downturned into a frown as the gist of the article dawned on her. '"Will these star-crossed lovers find happiness off the dance floor?"'

she quoted, and then shook her head. 'Goodness,' she murmured faintly.

'I'm sorry. Press were forbidden from coming to the
ball. I had no idea something like this would happen.'

'I had no idea our engagement seven years ago was so
well known,' Sierra said slowly. 'I thought it had been a
quiet affair.'

'Not that quiet. Your father made a public announce-
ment at a board meeting. It was in the papers.'

'Of course. It was business to him. And to you.' She
spoke without rancour, and Marco let the comment pass.

The last thing he wanted to talk about now was what
had happened all those years ago. He wanted to take Sierra back to bed and he wanted, he knew, for her to stay
past this afternoon.

Sierra took a deep breath and turned to face him directly. 'Do you mind? About the article?'

'It's an annoyance. I value my privacy, and yours, as
well.'

'Yes, but…' She hesitated, fiddling with the sash of
her robe. 'Having it all in the papers? The fact that I…
that I left you?'

Tension knotted between his shoulder blades. 'It's not
something I particularly relish having bandied about,' he
answered, keeping his voice mild with effort. 'But I'm not
heartbroken, Sierra.' He'd refused to be.

'Of course not,' she murmured and then nodded slowly.
'I should get ready for my flight.'

'Don't.' The word came out abruptly, a command he
hadn't intended to give.

She gazed at him, her eyebrows raised. 'Don't?'

'Don't get ready for your flight. Don't go on your flight.'
He held her gaze, willing her to agree.

'But the opening is over, Marco. I'm not needed here any more.'

'Not needed, maybe.' He paused, trying to find the right words. 'We're having fun, though, aren't we?'

Her gaze widened. 'Fun…'

'Why should we end it so soon?' Smiling, he reached for the sash of her robe and tugged on it gently, pulling her towards him. She went, a small smile curving her lips, and triumph roared through him. 'Stay with me,' he said when she'd come close enough for him to slide his hands under her robe, around her waist. Her skin was warm and silky soft. She let out a breathy little gasp of pleasure. 'Stay with me a little while longer.'

'I have a job, you know,' she reminded him, but she didn't sound as if it mattered much.

'Teaching a few after-school lessons? Can't you re-schedule?'

She frowned slightly but didn't move away. 'Maybe.'

'Then reschedule.' He pulled her close enough so their hips collided and she could feel how much he wanted her. 'Reschedule, and come with me to LA.' A few more days with her, nights with her, and then perhaps he'd have had enough. Perhaps then he'd be willing to let her go.

It was amazing how tempted she was, and yet not amazing at all because what woman on earth could resist Marco Ferranti when his hands were on her skin and his smile was so seductive?

And yet…to leave her job, her obligations, her life back in London and go with him wherever he beckoned?

'Sierra?' Marco brushed her neck with his lips in a kiss that promised so much more. 'You will come?' He nibbled lightly on her neck and Sierra let out a helpless gasp of pleasure as she reached up to clutch his shoulders so she could steady herself.

'Yes,' she managed, knowing there had never really been any doubt. 'Yes, I'll come with you.'

Later, lying amidst the tangled sheets while she admired the view of Marco's bare and perfect chest, Sierra finally summoned the mental energy to ask, 'Why are you going to LA?'

'I'm hoping to open the next North American Rocci hotel there.'

'Hoping?' Lazily, she ran her hand down the sculpted muscles of his chest, her fingers tracing the ridge of his abdomen before daring to dip lower.

Marco trapped her hand. 'Minx. Wait a few minutes, at least.'

'A few minutes?' Sierra teased. 'And here I thought you were some super stallion with superhero capabilities in the bedroom.'

'I've just proved my capabilities in the bedroom,' Marco growled as he rolled her over so he was on top of her, trapping her with his body. 'But I'll gladly prove it again.'

She smiled up at him, feeling sated and relaxed and happy. Happier than she'd been in a long time, perhaps ever. 'So have you started plans for a hotel in LA?'

'Preliminary plans.' Marco released her, rolling onto his back, but he kept one hand lying on her stomach and Sierra found she liked it. She'd had so few loving touches in her life. Her mother had hugged her on occasion, and her father only in public, but to be caressed and petted and stroked. She felt like a cat. She could almost start purring.

'What's got you looking like the cat who's just eaten the cream?' Marco asked as he shot her an amused look and Sierra laughed.

'I was just comparing myself to a cat, as it happens.'

'Comparing yourself to a cat? Why?'

'Because I like being touched. I feel like I could start purring.'

'And I like touching you.' Marco moved his hand from her stomach to her breasts and then Sierra almost did start purring. 'Very much.'

They spent the day in bed. Although not technically in bed; some time around noon Marco ordered food in and they ate it downstairs in the living area, in their dressing gowns. And some time in the late afternoon Marco ran a deep bath full of scented bubbles and just as Sierra was about to sink into all that bliss he actually joined her.

Water sloshed out of the tub as Sierra scooted to one side and Marco settled himself comfortably, seeming undaunted by the bubbles that clung to his chest.

'I didn't realise you were going to get in with me,' Sierra exclaimed, her voice coming out in a near squeak, and Marco arched an eyebrow.

'Is that a problem?'

'No, but…' How could she explain how it felt even more intimate to share a bath with this man than what they'd done in the privacy of the bedroom? And the things they'd done…

Quickly, Sierra realised she was being ridiculous. 'No, of course not,' she said and slid over so she was next to Marco, their legs tangling under the water. 'Actually, I can think of some interesting ways to wash.'

His gaze became hooded and sleepy as he watched her reach for the soap. 'Can you?'

'Oh, yes.' Her embarrassment and uncertainty, after a day's worth of thorough lovemaking, had fallen away. She felt confident, powerful in her knowledge of how much Marco desired her. 'Yes, indeed,' she murmured and she slid her soapy hands down his chest to his hips. After everything they'd done together that day she was amazed that Marco still desired her. But how could she be amazed, when she still desired him?

'Sierra…' His voice came out on a groan as she stroked his shaft. She loved giving him pleasure, loved knowing that she made him this way.

'You're going to kill me,' he muttered and stayed her hand.

She arched an eyebrow. 'But wouldn't it be a good way to go?'

'Yes indeed, but I have a lot more life in me yet,' he answered, and then showed her just how much.

Twilight was falling over the city several hours later as Sierra lay in bed and watched Marco get dressed. 'Are we going somewhere?' she asked as he pulled on a crisply ironed dress shirt.

'I have a business meeting,' he said with one swift, apologetic look towards her. 'It's been wonderful playing hookey today, but I've got to make back sometime.'

'Oh.' Sierra pulled the rumpled duvet over her naked body. 'Of course. So you're going out?'

'You can order whatever you like from room service,' Marco said as he selected a cobalt-blue tie.

Sierra watched him slide his tie in his collar and knot it with crisp, precise movements. She felt uneasy, almost hurt, and she wasn't quite sure why. Of course Marco had business meetings. Of course she couldn't tag along with him, nor would she want to.

'So.' He turned back to her with a quick smile that didn't reach his eyes. 'I'll see you later tonight. And tomorrow we'll go to LA.'

'I haven't even dealt with my plane ticket…'

'I cancelled it.'

She jerked back a little. 'You did?'

Marco was sliding on his jacket and checking his watch. 'Why should you worry about it?'

'But I need to book an alternative return flight…'

He gave her a wolfish smile. 'We don't need to think about that now.' Then he was dropping a distracted kiss on her forehead and hurrying out of the suite, all while she lay curled up in a crumpled duvet and wondered what she'd got herself into.

'A fling,' she said aloud. Her voice sounded small in the huge empty suite. 'You know very well what this is. A fling. You're here for sex.' What had seemed simple and safe now only felt sordid.

She got out of bed, trying to shake off her uncertain and grey mood, and dressed. She didn't feel like ordering takeaway and eating it alone upstairs; she'd go out, explore the city on her own for a bit.

Twenty minutes later Sierra headed downstairs and out of the modern glass doors of the hotel. The foyer was buzzing with guests; clearly the opening had been a success. A few people clearly recognised her, but Sierra ignored their speculative looks. She wasn't going to care about the tabloid article that had come out this morning. It would be forgotten by tomorrow, no doubt.

She strolled down Central Park West towards Columbus Circle, enjoying the way twilight settled on the city and the traffic started to die down. She found a little French bistro tucked onto a side street and went inside. As she sat down and glanced at the menu she realised she was ravenous. She supposed that was what making love all day did to you, and the thought made her smile. She ordered a steak and chips and ate it all and was just heading back outside, feeling replete and happy, when a reporter accosted her.

'Excuse me… Sierra Rocci?'

'Yes?' she answered automatically, before the flashbulb

popped in her face, making her momentarily blind, and the reporter started firing questions.

'Why are you out alone? Have you and Marco Ferranti had a lovers' tiff? Is it true you're staying in the same suite? Why did you jilt him seven years ago—'

'No comment,' Sierra gasped out and hurried away. The reporter kept yelling his awful questions at her, each one sounding like a horrible taunt.

'Did Ferranti cheat on you? Did you cheat on him? Are you together now merely as a business arrangement?'

Finally Sierra rounded the corner and the reporter's questions died away. She kept up a brisk pace all the way to the hotel, only slowing when she came to the front steps. Her heart was thudding and she felt clammy with sweat. She'd thought she could handle the press, but she hadn't been prepared for that.

She'd managed to restore her composure by the time she got into the penthouse lift, and she felt almost normal when the doors opened.

That was until she stepped out and Marco loomed in front of her, his face thunderous, his voice a harsh demand.

'Where the *hell* have you been?'

CHAPTER FOURTEEN

MARCO COULDN'T REMEMBER the last time he'd felt so furious—and so afraid. He'd come up to the penthouse suite expecting to see Sierra still lounging in bed, waiting for him. Instead, the place had been echoing and empty, and when he'd called downstairs the concierge had said she'd left hours ago.

He'd paced the penthouse for a quarter of an hour, trying to stifle his panic and anger, but rational thought was hard when so many memories kept crowding in. He told himself she hadn't taken her clothes and that she wouldn't just leave.

But she'd taken hardly anything when she'd left the night before his wedding. And the possibility that she might have skipped out on him again made everything in him clench. Damn it, he would be the one to say when they were done. And it wasn't yet.

'Well?' he demanded while she simply stared at him. 'Do you have an answer?'

'No,' Sierra stated clearly, her voice so very cold, and she stalked past him.

Marco whirled around, disbelieving. '*No?* You're gone for hours and you can't even tell me where you went?'

'I don't have to tell you anything, Marco,' Sierra tossed over her shoulder. 'I don't owe you anything.'

'How about an explanation?'

She walked up the spiral stairs, one hand on the railing, her head held high. 'Not even that.'

Marco followed her up the stairs and into the bedroom and then watched in disbelief as she took out her suitcase and started putting clothes into it.

'You're packing?'

She gave him a grim smile. 'It looks like it, doesn't it?'

'For LA?'

She stilled and then raised her head, her gaze clear and direct. 'No. For London.'

Fury and hurt coursed through him, choking him so he could barely speak. He didn't want to feel hurt; anger was stronger. 'Damn it, Sierra,' he exclaimed. He raised his hand to do what, he didn't know—touch her shoulder, beseech her somehow—but he stilled when she instinctively flinched as if she'd expected him to strike her.

'Sierra?' His voice was low, her name a question.

She straightened, her expression erased of the cringing fear he'd seen for one alarming second. 'I'm going.'

Marco watched her for a few moments, forcing himself to be calm. He'd overreacted; he could see that now. 'Were you planning on returning to London before you got back to the penthouse?' he asked quietly.

She gave him another one of those direct looks that cut right to his heart. 'No, I wasn't.'

He took a deep breath and then let it out slowly. 'I'm sorry I was so angry.'

She made a tiny shrugging gesture, as if it was of no importance, and yet Marco knew instinctively that it was. 'You flinched just then, almost as if…' He didn't want to voice the suspicion lurking in the dark corners of his mind. And maybe that flinch had been a moment's instinctive reaction, and yet…she'd had such a look on her face, one of terrible fear.

'Almost as if what?' Sierra asked, and it sounded like a challenge.

'Almost as if you expected me to…' He swallowed hard. 'Hit you.'

'I wasn't,' she said after a moment. She took a deep breath and let it out slowly. 'But old habits die hard, I suppose.'

'What do you mean?'

She sighed and shook her head. 'There's no point having this conversation.'

'How can you say that? This might be the most important conversation we've ever had.'

'Oh, Marco.' She looked up at him, and everything in him jolted at the look of weary sorrow in her eyes. 'I wish it could be, but…' She trailed off, biting her lip.

'What do you mean? What aren't you telling me?' She didn't answer and he forced himself not to take a step towards her, not to raise his voice or seem threatening in any way. 'Sierra, did a man…did a man ever hit you?'

The silence following his question seemed endless. Marco felt as if he could scarcely breathe.

Finally Sierra looked up, resignation in every weary line of her lovely face. 'Yes,' she said and then Marco felt a fury like none he'd known before—this time at this unknown man who had dared to hurt and abuse her. He'd *kill* the bastard.

'Who?' he demanded. 'A boyfriend…?'

'No,' she said flatly. 'My father.'

Sierra watched Marco blink, his jaw slackening, as he stared at her in obvious disbelief. She kept packing. Having him yell at her like that had been the wake-up call she needed, and in that moment she'd realised why she'd felt so uneasy earlier, when Marco had left her alone in the suite. She was turning into her mother. Dropping her own life at a man's request, living for his pleasure. There was no way she was walking even one step down that road, and when Marco had shouted at her, looking so angry, Sierra had realised the trap she'd been just about to step into. Thank God she'd realised before it was too late... even if the thought of leaving Marco made her insides twist with grief.

'Your father?' Marco repeated hoarsely. 'Arturo? No.'

'I knew you wouldn't believe me.'

He was shaking his head slowly, looking utterly winded. Sierra almost felt sorry for him.

'But...' he began, and then stopped. She reached for the dress she'd worn to the opening yesterday. 'Sierra, wait.' He grabbed her wrist, gently but firmly, and she went completely still.

He stared at her for a moment, his face white, and then he let her go and backed away, his hands raised like a man about to be arrested. 'You know I would never, ever hurt you.'

'I know that,' she said quietly. She believed it but even with that head knowledge she couldn't keep from fearing. Trust was a hard, hard thing.

Slowly, Marco dropped his hands. Sierra resumed packing. He watched her for several moments and his scrutiny made her hands tremble as she tried to fold her clothes. 'Do you mind?' she finally asked, and to her irritation her voice shook.

'What did you mean—that he hit you?' Marco asked.

'Does it really need explaining?'

'Sierra, your father was as good as my father. I loved him. I trusted him. Yes, it needs explaining.' His voice came out harsh, grating, and she forced herself not to flinch.

'Then let me explain it for you,' she said coolly. She was surprised at how much a relief it was to tell him the truth. She'd been keeping this secret for far too long, first out of fear that he wouldn't believe her, and then because she hadn't wanted to hurt him. Both reasons seemed like pathetic excuses now. 'My father hit me,' Sierra stated clearly. 'Often. He hit my mother, too. He played the doting father and adoring husband for the public, but in private he heaped physical and emotional abuse on us. Slaps, pinches, punches, the lot. And the words…the insults, the sneers, the mockery.' She shook her head, tears stinging her eyes as a lump formed in her throat. 'My mother loved him anyway. I've never been able to understand that. She loved him and wouldn't hear a word against him, although she always tried to protect me from his anger.'

Marco was shaking his head, his body language refuting every word she'd said. 'No…'

'I don't care if you believe me or not,' Sierra said, even though she knew that for a lie. She did care. Far too much. 'But at least now I've said it. Now you know, even if you don't want to.'

She closed her suitcase, struggling with the zip. Marco placed a hand on top of the case. 'Please, Sierra, don't go like this.'

'Why should I stay?'

'Because I want you to stay. Because we've been having a fantastic time.' He took a deep breath. 'Look, this is a tremendous shock to me. It's not that I don't believe you, but give me a few moments to absorb it. Please.'

Slowly Sierra nodded. She could see the sense in what he was staying, even if her instinct was to run. And in truth there was a part of her, a large part, that didn't want to leave. 'Okay,' she said, and then waited.

A full minute passed in silence. Finally Marco said hesitantly, 'Why…why didn't you tell me?'

'Would you have believed me? You hated me, Marco.' It hurt to remind him of that.

'I mean before.' The look he gave her was full of confusion and pain, and it made guilt flash through her like a streak of lightning. 'When we were engaged.'

'Even then you were his right-hand man.'

'But you were going to marry me. How could we have had a marriage, with such a secret between us?'

'I realised we couldn't.'

'Your *father* is why you left?' Marco stared at her in disbelief, his jaw tight.

'In a manner of speaking, I suppose.'

'I don't understand, Sierra.' He raked his hands through his hair and even now, in the midst of all this confusion and misery, Sierra watched him with longing. Those muscled arms had held her so tenderly. She'd nestled against that chiselled chest, had kissed his salty skin. She averted her gaze from him. 'Please help me to understand,' Marco said, and underneath the sadness Sierra heard a note of frustration, even anger, and she tensed.

'I don't know what you want me to say.'

'Anything. Something. Why did you agree to marry me?' The question rang out, echoing through the suite.

Sierra took a deep breath and met his gaze. 'To get away from my father.'

Marco's face paled as his jaw bunched. Sierra kept herself from flinching even though she could tell he was angry. She didn't completely understand why, but she felt it emanating from his taut body. 'That's the only reason?' he asked in a low voice.

Wordlessly she nodded, and then she watched as Marco turned and strode from the bedroom. Alone, she sank onto the bed, her legs suddenly feeling weak. Everything feeling weak. She felt nearer to tears now than she had a few moments ago, and why? Because she'd lost Marco? It was better this way, and in any case she'd never really had him. Not like that.

But it still felt like a loss, a gaping wound that was bleeding out. Another deep breath and Sierra turned to her suitcase. She struggled with the zip, but she finally got it closed. And then she sat there, having no idea what to do. Where to go, if anywhere.

After a few moments she worked up the nerve to lug her suitcase down the spiral staircase. Marco stood in the living room, his back to her as he stared out at the darkened city. She hesitated on the bottom step because now that she was here, she didn't really want to go. Walk out like she did once before, into a dark night, an unknown future.

Yet how could she stay?

The step creaked beneath her and Marco turned around, his dark eyebrows snapping together as he saw her clutching the handle of her suitcase. 'You're still planning to go?' he asked, his voice harsh.

'I don't know what to do, Marco.' She hated the wobble in her voice and she blinked rapidly. Marco swore under his breath and strode towards her.

'Sierra, *cara*, I've been an utter ass. Please forgive me.'

It was the last thing she'd expected him to say. He took the suitcase from her and put it on the floor. Then he stretched out his hands beseechingly, his face a plea. 'Don't go, Sierra. Please. Not yet. Not till I understand. Not till we've made this right.'

'How can we? I know what my father meant to you, and I hate him, *hate* him—' She broke off, weeping, half amazed at the emotion that suddenly burst from her, tears trickling down her cheeks. 'I always have,' she continued, but then her voice was lost to sobs, her shoulders shaking, and Marco had enfolded her in his arms.

She pressed her face into his hard chest as he stroked his hand down her back and murmured nonsense endearments. She hadn't realised she had so many tears left in her and, more than just tears, a deep welling of grief and sorrow, not just for the father she'd had, but for the father she'd never had. For the years of loneliness and fear and frustration. For the fact that even now, seven years on, she was afraid to trust someone. To love someone, and the result was this brokenness, this feeling that she might never be whole.

'I'm sorry,' she finally managed, pulling away from him a bit to swipe at her damp cheeks. Now that the first storm of crying had passed, she felt embarrassed by her emotional display. 'I didn't mean to fall apart...'

'Nonsense. You needed to cry. You have suffered, Sierra, more than I could ever imagine. More than I ever knew.' Sierra heard the sharp note of self-recrimination in Marco's voice and wondered at it. 'Come, let us sit down.'

He guided her to one of the leather sofas and pulled her down next to him, his arm around her shoulders so she was still nestled against him, safe in his arms. Neither of them spoke for a long moment.

'Will you tell me?' Marco finally asked.

Sierra drew a shuddering breath. 'What do you want to know?'

'Everything.'

'I don't know where to begin.'

He nestled her closer to him, settling them both more comfortably. 'Begin wherever you want to, Sierra,' he said quietly.

After a moment she started talking, searching for each word, finding her way slowly. She told him how the first time her father hit her she was four years old, a slap across the face, and she hadn't understood what she'd done wrong. It had taken her decades to realise the answer to that question: nothing.

She told him about how kind and jovial he could be, throwing her up in the air, calling her his princess, showering her and her mother with gifts. 'It wasn't until I was much older that I realised he only treated us that way when someone was watching.'

'And when you were alone?' Marco asked in a low voice. 'Always…?'

'Often enough so that I tried to hide from him, but that angered him, too. No monster likes to see his reflection.'

'And when you were older?'

'I knew I needed to get away. My mother would never leave him. I begged her to, but she refused. She'd get quite angry with me because she loved him.' Sierra shook her head slowly. 'I've never understood that. I know he could be charming and he was handsome, but the way he treated her…' Her voice choked and she sniffed loudly.

'So why didn't you run away? When you were older?'

She let out an abrupt yet weary laugh. 'You make it sound so simple.'

'I don't mean to,' Marco answered. 'I just want to understand. It all seems so difficult to believe.'

How difficult? Sierra wondered. *Did* he believe her? Or even now did he doubt? The possibility was enough to make her fall silent. Marco touched her chin with his finger, turning her face so she had to look at him.

'I didn't mean it like that, Sierra.'

'Do you believe me?' she blurted. The question felt far

too revealing, and even worse was Marco's silence after she'd asked it.

'Yes,' he said finally. 'Of course I do. But I don't want to.'

'Because you loved him.'

Marco nodded, his expression shuttered, his jaw tight. 'You know how I told you my own father left? He was hardly around to begin with, and then one day he just never came back. And my mother...' He paused, and curiosity flared within the misery that had swamped her.

'Your mother?'

'It doesn't matter. What I meant to say is that Arturo was the closest thing to a father that I ever had. I told you how I was working as a bellboy when he noticed me... I would have spent my life heaving suitcases if not for him. He took me out for a drink, told me he could tell I had ambition and drive. Then he gave me a job as an office junior when I was seventeen. Within a few years he'd promoted me, and you know the rest.' He sighed, his arm still around her. 'And all the while he'd encourage me, listen to me... accept me in a way my father never did. To now realise this man I held in such high esteem was...was what you say he was...' Marco's voice turned hoarse. 'It hurts to believe it. But I do.'

'Thank you,' she whispered.

'You don't need to thank me, Sierra.' He paused, and Sierra could tell he was searching for words. 'So you wanted to escape. Why did you choose me?'

'My father chose you,' Sierra returned. 'I was under no illusion about that, although I flattered myself to think I had a bit more discernment and control than I actually did.' She let out a sad, soft laugh. 'Do you know what convinced me, Marco? I saw you stroking a cat, the day I met you. You were in the courtyard, waiting to come in, and one of the street cats wound its way between your legs. You bent down and stroked it. My father would have kicked it away. In that moment I believed you were a gentle man.'

'You sound,' Marco said after a moment, 'as if you now think you were wrong.'

'No, I...' She stopped, biting her lip. It was so difficult to separate what she'd felt then and what she felt now. 'I was going to marry you for the wrong reasons, Marco, back then. I realised that the night before our wedding. No matter what is between us now—and I know it's just a fling—it would have never worked back then. I needed to find my own way, become my own person.'

'So what happened that night?' Marco asked. 'Really?' He sounded as if he were struggling with some emotion, perhaps anger. Sierra could feel how tense his body was.

'Just what I told you. I overheard you talking with my father. I realised just how close you were. I...I hadn't quite realised it before. And then I heard my father give you that awful advice.'

'"I know how to handle her",' Marco repeated flatly. 'I see now why that would have alarmed you, but...couldn't you have asked me, Sierra?'

'And what would I ask, exactly?' The first note of temper entered her voice. '"Will you ever hit me, Marco?" That's not exactly a question someone will answer honestly.'

'I would have.'

'I wouldn't have believed you. That's what I realised that night, Marco. I was taking too great a risk. It was about me as much as it was about you.'

'So you ran away, just as you could have done before we'd ever become engaged.'

'Not exactly. My mother helped me. When I told her I didn't love you...' Sierra trailed off uncertainly. Of course

Marco knew she hadn't loved him then. He hadn't loved her. And yet it sounded so cold now.

'Yes? When you told her that, what did she do?'

'She gave me some money,' Sierra whispered. 'And the name of a friend in England I could go to.'

'And you just walked out into the night? Into Palermo?'

'Yes. I was terrified.' She swallowed hard, the memories swarming her. 'Utterly terrified. I'd never been out alone in the city—any city—before. But I hailed a taxi and went to the docks. I waited the rest of the night in the ferry office, and then I took the first boat to the mainland.'

'And then to England? That must have been quite a journey.' Marco didn't sound impressed so much as incredulous.

'Yes, it was. I took endless trains, and then I was spat out in London with barely enough English to make myself understood. I got lost on the Tube and someone tried to pickpocket me. And when I went to find my mother's friend, she'd moved house. I spent a night at a women's shelter and then used a computer in a library to locate the new address of my mother's friend, and she finally took me in.'

'So much effort to get away from me,' Marco remarked tonelessly and Sierra jerked away from him.

'No, to get away from my father. It wasn't about you, Marco. I keep telling you that.'

He gazed at her with eyes the colour of steel, his mouth a hard line. 'How can you say that, Sierra? It most certainly was about me. Yes, it was about your father, as well, I understand that. But if you'd known me at all, if you'd trusted me at all, you would never have had to go to London.'

She recognised the truth of his words even if she didn't want to. 'Understandably,' she answered stiffly, 'I have had difficulties with trusting people, especially men.'

Marco sighed, the sound one of defeat, his shoulders slumping. 'Understandably,' he agreed quietly. 'Yes.'

Sierra stood up, pacing the room, her arms wrapped around her body. Suddenly she felt cold. She had no idea if what she'd told Marco changed things. Then she realised that of course it changed things; she had no idea how much.

'What now?' she finally asked, and she turned to face him. He was still sitting on the sofa, watching her, his expression bland. 'Should I leave?' she forced herself to ask. 'I can go back to London tonight.'

Marco didn't look away; he didn't so much as blink. 'Is that what you want?'

Was it? Her heart hammered and her mouth went dry. Here was a moment when she could try to trust. When she could leap out and see if he caught her. If he wanted to. 'No,' she whispered. 'It isn't.'

Marco looked startled, and then a look of such naked relief passed over his face that Sierra sagged with a deep relief of her own.

He rose from the sofa and crossed the room, pulling her into his arms. 'Good,' he said, and kissed her.

CHAPTER FIFTEEN

MARCO GAZED OUT at the azure sky, his eyes starting to water from staring at its hard brightness for so long. The plane was minutes away from touching down in LA and he'd barely spoken to Sierra for the six hours of the flight.

He'd wanted to. He'd formed a dozen different conversation openers in his mind, but everything sounded wrong in his head. He had a feeling it would sound worse out loud. The trouble was, since her revelation last night he hadn't known how to approach her. *How to handle her.*

Guilt churned in his stomach as he replayed in his mind all that Sierra had told him. It was a form of self-torture he couldn't keep himself from indulging in. A thousand conflicting thoughts and feelings tormented him: sadness for what Sierra had endured, guilt for his part in it, confusion and grief for what he'd felt for Arturo, a man he'd loved but who had been a monster beyond his worst imaginings.

In the end, beyond a few basic pleasantries about the trip and their destination, he'd stayed silent, and so had Sierra. It seemed easier, even if it made him an emotional coward.

'Please fasten your seat belts as we prepare for landing.'

Marco glanced at Sierra, trying for a reassuring smile. She smiled back but he could see that it didn't reach her eyes, which were the colour of the Atlantic on a cold day.

Wintry grey-blue, no thaw in sight. Was she angry at him? Did she blame him somehow for what had happened before? How on earth were they going to get past this?

Which begged another question—one he was reluctant to answer, even to himself. Why did they need to get past this? What kind of future was he envisioning with Sierra?

A few days ago he'd wanted to be the one to walk away first. But a realisation was emerging amidst all his confusion and regret—he didn't want to walk away at all.

But how could they build a relationship on such shaky, crumbling foundations of mistrust and betrayal? And how could he even want to, when he had no idea what Sierra wanted? When he'd been so sure he'd never love someone, never want to love someone?

'Are you looking forward to seeing Los Angeles?' he asked abruptly, wanting to break the glacial silence as well as keep from the endless circling of his own thoughts.

'Yes, thank you,' Sierra replied, and her tone was just as carefully polite. They were acting like strangers, yet maybe, after all they hadn't known about each other, they *were* strangers.

The next hour was taken up with deplaning and then retrieving their luggage; Marco had arranged for a limo to be waiting outside.

Once they'd slid inside its luxurious leather depths, the soundproof glass cocooning them in privacy, the silence felt worse. More damning.

And still neither of them spoke.

'Where are we staying?' Sierra finally asked as the limo headed down I-405. 'Since there isn't a Rocci hotel here yet?'

'The Beverly Wilshire.' He managed a small smile. 'I need to check out my competition.'

'Of course.' She turned back to the window, her gaze

on the palm trees and billboards lining the highway. The silence stretched on.

Sierra admired the impressive Art Deco foyer of the hotel, and when a bellboy escorted them to the private floor that housed the penthouse suite, Marco experienced a little dart of satisfaction at how awed she looked. It might not be a Rocci hotel, but he could still give her the best. He wanted to give her the best.

And the penthouse suite *was* the best: three bedrooms, four marble bathrooms, a media room, plus the usual dining room, living room and kitchen. But best of all was the spacious terrace with its panoramic views of the city.

Sierra stepped out onto the terrace, breathed in the hot, dry air of the desert. She glanced up at the scrubby hills that bordered Los Angeles to the north. 'It almost looks like Sicily.'

'Almost,' Marco agreed.

'I don't know if we need such a big suite,' she said with a small teasing smile. 'Three bedrooms?'

'We can sleep in a different one each night.'

Her smile faltered. 'How long are you planning on staying here?'

Marco noted the 'you' and deliberately kept his voice even and mild. 'I'm not sure. I want to complete the preliminary negotiations for The Rocci Los Angeles, and I don't need to be back in Palermo until next week.' He shrugged. 'We might as well stay and enjoy California.' *Enjoy each other.* He only just kept himself from saying it.

'I have a job to get back to,' Sierra reminded him. 'A life.'

And she was telling him this why? 'You have a freelance job,' Marco pointed out. 'What is that if not flexible?'

Her eyebrows drew together and she looked away. So he'd said the wrong thing. He'd known he would all along.

Sierra walked back into the suite and after a moment Marco followed. When he came into the living area he saw how lost she looked, how forlorn.

'I think I might take a bath,' she said without looking at him. 'Wash away the travel grime.'

'All right,' Marco answered, and in frustration he watched her walk out of the room.

Could things get more awkward and horrible? With a grimace Sierra turned the taps of the huge sunken marble tub on full blast. She didn't know what she regretted more: telling Marco the truth about her father or coming with him to LA. The trouble was, she still wanted to be with him. She just didn't know how they were going to get past this seeming roadblock in their relationship.

Whoa. You don't have a relationship.

She might be halfway to falling in love with him, but that didn't mean Marco felt the same. He'd made it abundantly clear that they were only having a fling and, in any case, she didn't even *want* him to feel the same. She didn't want to be in love herself. Not when she'd seen what it had done to her mother. Not when she'd felt what it could do to herself.

Since meeting Marco again her whole world had been tangled up in knots. Since making love with him she'd felt happier and yet more frightened than she ever had in the last seven years. Happiness could be so fleeting, so fragile, and yet, once discovered, so unbearably necessary. How much was it going to hurt when Marco was gone from her life?

Better to make a quick, clean cut. She'd told herself that yesterday and yet here she was. She was more like her mother than she'd ever wanted to be. Filled with regret and uncertainty, Sierra closed her eyes.

She almost didn't hear the gentle tapping at the bathroom door. She opened her eyes, alert, and then heard Marco call softly, 'Sierra? May I come in?'

She glanced down at her naked body, covered by bubbles. Everything in her seemed to both hesitate and yearn.

'All right,' she said.

Slowly the door opened. Marco stepped inside the steamy bathroom; he'd changed his business suit for faded jeans and a black T-shirt that clung to his chest. His hair was rumpled, his jaw shadowed with stubble, his eyes dark and serious.

'I haven't known what to say to you.'

Sierra gazed at him with wide eyes. She felt intensely vulnerable lying naked in the bath, and yet she recognised that Marco had come in here for a reason. An important reason. 'I haven't known what to say, either.'

'I wish I had the right words.'

'So do I,' she whispered.

Slowly Marco came towards her. Sierra watched him, her breath held, her heart beating hard. 'May I help you wash?' he asked and she stared at him, paralysed by indecision and longing. Finally, wordlessly, she nodded.

She watched as Marco reached for the bar of expensive soap the hotel provided and lathered his hands. He motioned for her to lean forward and after a moment she did and he began to soap her back. His touch was gentle, almost hesitant, and it felt loving. It also felt incredibly intimate, even more so than the things they'd done together in bed. Yet there was nothing overtly sexual about his touch as he slid his hands up and down her back. It felt almost as if he were offering some kind of penance, asking for absolution. Almost as if this act was as intimate and revealing for him as it was for her.

She let out a shuddering breath as he pressed a kiss

to the back of her neck. Desire, like liquid fire, spread through her as he kissed his way down the knobs of her spine.

'Marco…'

'Let me make love to you, Sierra.'

She nodded her assent and in one easy movement he scooped her up from the tub and, cradling her in his arms, he brought her back to the master bedroom. Sierra gazed up at him with huge eyes as he laid her down on the bed and then stripped his clothes from his body.

She held her arms out and he went to her, covering her body with his own, kissing her with a raw urgency she hadn't felt from him before. And she responded in kind, kiss for kiss, touch for touch, both of them rushed and desperate for each other, until Marco finally sank inside her, buried deep, her name a sob in his throat as they climaxed together.

Afterwards they lay quietly as their heart rates returned to normal and honeyed sunlight filtered through the curtains.

She would miss this, Sierra thought, when it was over. And despite the tenderness Marco had just shown her, despite the fierce pleasure of their lovemaking, she knew it would be over soon. She felt it in the way Marco had already withdrawn back into the shuttered privacy of his thoughts, his eyebrows drawn together as he stared up at the ceiling. She had no idea what he was thinking or feeling. Moments ago he'd been the most loving, gentle man she could have imagined, and now?

She sighed and stirred from the bed. 'I should dress.'

He barely glanced at her as he reached for his clothes. 'We can order room service if you like.'

'I'd rather go out.' She wanted to escape the oppressive silence that had plagued them both since last night.

'Very well,' Marco answered, and he didn't look at her as he started to dress.

An hour later they were seated at an upmarket sea-food restaurant off Rodeo Drive. Sierra perused the extensive and exotic menu while Marco frowned down at the wine list.

'So what business do you have to do here exactly?' she asked after they'd both ordered.

'I'm meeting with the real estate developers to agree on the site for the new hotel.'

'Where is it?'

'Not far from here. A vacant lot off Wilshire Boulevard.' He drummed his fingers on the table, seeming almost impatient, and Sierra couldn't help but feel nettled.

'Sorry, am I wasting your time?' she asked tartly and Marco turned to her, startled.

'No, of course not.'

'It's just you seem like you can't wait to get away.'

'*I* seem…?' Now he looked truly flummoxed. 'No, of course not.'

Sierra didn't answer. Maybe the problem was with her, not with Marco. She could feel how his changing moods affected her, made her both worry and want to please him. Had her mother been like this, wondering if her husband would come home smiling or screaming? Bracing herself for a kiss or a kick?

She couldn't stand the see-sawing of emotions in herself, in Marco. The endless uncertainty. It had been better before, when she hadn't cared so much. That was the problem, Sierra realised. She really was starting to love him. Maybe she already did.

Cold fear clawed at her. *So much for a fling.* How had she let this happen? How had he slipped under her defences and reached her heart, despite everything? She'd never wanted love, never looked for it, and yet it had found her anyway.

'Is something wrong?'

Sierra jerked her gaze up to Marco's narrowed one. 'No...'

'It's just that you're frowning.'

'Sorry.' She shook her head, managed a rather sick smile. 'I'm just tired, I suppose.'

Marco regarded her quietly, clearly unconvinced by her lie. 'My business should only take a few days,' he said. 'I'll be done by the day after tomorrow. Maybe then we could go somewhere. Palm Desert...'

For a second Sierra imagined it: staying in a luxurious resort, days of being pampered and nights spent in Marco's arms. And then, after a few days, what would happen? Maybe he would ask her to go with him to Palermo. Maybe there would be more shopping trips and fancy restaurants and gala events. But eventually he would tire of her tagging along with him, leaving her own life far behind, just as her mother had. And even if he didn't tire of her, what would she be but a plaything, a pawn?

And yet still she was tempted. *This was what love did to you.* It wrecked you completely, emotionally, physically— everything. It took and took and took and gave nothing back.

Marco frowned as he noted her lack of response. 'Sierra?'

'How long would we go to Palm Desert for?'

Marco shrugged. 'I don't know—a few days? I told you, I have to be back in Palermo next week.'

'Right.' And never mind what she had to do. Of course. Sierra took a deep breath. This felt like the hardest thing she'd ever said, and yet she knew it had to be done. 'I don't think so, Marco.'

His mouth tightened and his eyes flashed. She knew he'd taken her meaning completely. Before he could respond the waiter came with their wine, a bottle of champagne that now seemed like a mockery, the loud sound of the cork popping a taunt.

The waiter poured two flutes with a flourish, the fizz going right to the top. Marco took one of the flutes and raised it sardonically.

'So what shall we toast?'

Sierra could only shake her head. She felt swamped with misery, overwhelmed by it. She didn't want things with Marco to end like this, and yet she didn't know how else they could end. Any ending was bound to be brutal.

'To nothing, then,' Marco said, his voice hard and bitter, and drank.

CHAPTER SIXTEEN

HE WAS LOSING HER, and he couldn't even say he was surprised. This was what happened when you loved someone. They left.

And he loved Sierra. Had loved her for a long time. And even though he'd been telling himself he would walk away, Marco knew he didn't want to. Ever. He wanted to love Sierra, to go to sleep with her at night and wake up with her in the morning. To hold her in his arms, hold their child in his arms. To experience everything life had to offer, good and bad, with her.

Marco put down his empty champagne flute, his insides churning with the realisation. He loved Sierra and she was slipping away from him every second.

'I think perhaps I'm not hungry after all,' she said quietly. Her face was pale, her fingers trembling as she placed the napkin on the table and rose from her seat.

She was leaving him, in a public restaurant? The papers would have a field day. Quickly, Marco rose, taking her elbow as he steered her out of the restaurant.

She jerked away from him the moment they were out on the street. '*Don't* manhandle me.'

'Manhandle?' he repeated incredulously. 'There were bound to be reporters in there, Sierra. Paparazzi. I was just trying to get us out of there without a scene.'

She shook her head, rubbing her elbow as if he'd hurt her. He suddenly felt sick.

'You think I'd hurt you? After everything?'

'No,' she said, but she didn't sound convinced. She'd never trust him, Marco realised. Never mind love him. Not after everything that had happened with Arturo, and not with how close he'd been to the man. The memories ran too deep. No matter what either of them felt, they had no chance.

'Let's go back to the hotel,' he said tersely and hailed a cab.

Back at the penthouse suite, Sierra turned to face him. 'I think I should leave,' she said, voice wobbling and chin held high.

'At least you had the decency to tell me this time,' Marco answered before he could keep himself from it. He felt too emotionally raw to be measured or calm.

Her face paled but she simply nodded and turned away. He sank onto a sofa, his head in his hands, as he listened to her start to pack.

He told himself it was better this way. The past held too much power for them to ever have a real relationship, if that was even what Sierra wanted.

But it was what he wanted. What he needed. Was he really going to let Sierra walk out of his life a second time?

The force of his feelings felt like a hammer blow to his heart, leaving him breathless. He *loved* this woman, loved her too much to let her walk away. Again.

But that was what people did. His father, his mother, Sierra. They'd all left him, slipped out without saying goodbye, leaving him with nothing to do but wait and grieve.

But this time he had a choice. He had a chance to talk to Sierra honestly, to ask or even beg her to stay. He wouldn't be proud. He loved her too much for that. The realisation sent adrenaline coursing through him and he rose from the sofa, pacing the room as panic roared through him. What if she said no? What if she still left?

Sierra emerged from the bedroom, her face still pale, her suitcase clutched in one hand. 'I can call for a taxi…'

'Don't.' The word came out like a command, and far too aggressive. Sierra blinked, then set her jaw. She didn't like him ordering her around, and he could understand that. He respected it, liked her—no, *loved* her—more for it.

'Please,' he burst out. 'Sierra, I don't want you to walk out of my life again.'

She hesitated and he took the opportunity to walk towards her, take the suitcase from her unresisting hand. 'Please listen to me for just a few minutes. And if you still want to leave after I'm done, I won't stop you, I promise.' His voice was hoarse, his heart beating painfully hard.

Sierra nibbled her lip, her wide eyes searching his face, and then finally she nodded. 'All right,' she whispered.

He led her over to the sofa and she sat down but he found he couldn't. He had too much raw energy coursing through him for that. 'I don't want you to go,' he said as he paced in front of her. 'I don't want you to go today or tomorrow or the day after that.' The words burst from him, a confession that hurt even though he knew he needed to make it. For once in his life he was fighting for what he wanted, who he loved, and even in this moment of intense vulnerability it made him feel powerful. Strong. *Love* made him strong. 'I don't want you to go ever, Sierra.'

'It hasn't been working, Marco.' Her voice was soft and sad. 'There's too much history…'

'I know there is, but we're giving the past too much power.' He dropped to his knees in front of her and took her cold hands in his. 'I love you, Sierra. I only realised how much when you were about to walk out that door. I've been a fool and an ass and whatever other name you want to throw at me. I deserve it. When you told me about your father, I didn't know how to handle it. I felt guilty and hurt and betrayed all at once, and I was afraid you'd always associate me with him, you'd never be able to trust or love me. And maybe you won't but I want to try. I want to try with you. Not just a fling, but something real. A relationship. Marriage, children—the fairy tale if we can both believe in it.'

Tears sparkled in her eyes and she clung to his hands. 'I don't know if I can. My mother loved my father and look what it did to her. It killed her in the end, maybe not literally, but she was never the person she could have been. She was like a shadow, a ghost—'

'That wasn't love. Love builds up, not breaks down. I have to believe that. I want the best for you, Sierra—'

'To follow you around from one Rocci hotel to another?' she burst out. 'I don't want to live in your shadow, Marco.'

'And you don't have to. We can make this work. I realise your life in London is important. I won't ask you to drop it to follow me around. I want you to be happy, Sierra, but I want you to be happy with me. If you think you can.' He held his breath, waiting for her answer.

'I want to be,' she finally said, her voice hesitant.

'I know I've made a lot of mistakes. I've let the past affect me more than I wanted it to. Not just your leaving, but my father's. And...' He paused because this was something he'd never told another person '...my mother.'

Sierra frowned. 'Your mother?'

'She left when I was ten,' Marco admitted quietly. 'After my father walked out she tried to hold things together, but it was tough as a single mother in a conservative country. She ended up taking me to an orphanage in Palermo, run by monks. She said she'd come back for me, but she never did.'

Tears filled Sierra's eyes. 'Oh, Marco…'

'I stayed until I was sixteen, and then I got the job at The Rocci. I tried never to look back, but I've realised I was looking back all the time, letting the past affect me. Control me. That's why I took your leaving before so badly. Why I've been afraid to love anyone.'

She bit her lip, a single tear sliding down her cheek, devastating him. 'I've been afraid, too.'

Gently, Marco wiped the tear from her cheek. 'Then let's be afraid together. I know it might be hard and there will be arguments and fears and all the rest of it. But we can find the fairy tale, Sierra. Together. I believe that. I have to believe that.'

Sierra gazed at him, her eyes filled with tears and yet also a dawning wonder, a fragile hope. 'Yes,' she said. 'I believe that, too.' And then, as Marco's heart trembled with joy, she leaned forward and kissed him.

EPILOGUE

Three years later

SIERRA STOOD AT the window of their London townhouse and watched as Marco came inside, whistling under his breath. A smile softened her features as she watched him, loving how light and happy he looked. There had been so much happiness over the last three years.

Not, of course, that it had been easy or simple. She and Marco had both had so many fears and hurts to conquer. So many mountains to climb. And yet they'd climbed them, hand in hand, struggling and searching, together.

They'd married in a quiet ceremony two years ago, and then decided to split their time between Palermo and London; Sierra continued with her music teaching, using holiday time to travel with Marco to various hotels all over the world. The Rocci Los Angeles had opened last year and Marco already had plans to open another hotel in Montreal, although he'd promised to reduce his work schedule in the next few months.

'Sierra?' His voice floated up the stairs and Sierra called back.

'I'm in the nursery.'

Grinning, Marco appeared in the doorway, his warm glance resting on the gentle swell of Sierra's bump. They were expecting a baby girl in just over three months—a new generation, a wonderful way to redeem the past and forge a future together.

'You're feeling all right?' he asked as he came towards her.

Laughing, she shook her head. 'You don't have to coddle me, Marco.'

'I want to coddle you.' He slid his arms around her, resting his hands over her bump. She laced her fingers with his, savouring his gentle touch.

That had been another mountain to climb: forcing her fears back and trusting in Marco's love and goodness. And he'd been so good, so gentle and patient with her in so many ways. It had taken her a few years before she felt brave enough to start a family, to trust Marco not only with her own heart but the heart of their child's.

The reality of their baby, their joined flesh, had made their marriage all the stronger. Sierra had never looked back.

As if agreeing with her, their baby kicked beneath their joined hands. Marco laughed softly. 'I felt that one.'

'She's a strong one,' Sierra answered with a little laugh and leaned her head back against Marco's shoulder.

'Just like her mother, then,' Marco said, and kissed her.

* * * * *

MILLS & BOON®

Why shop at millsandboon.co.uk?

Each year, thousands of romance readers find their perfect read at millsandboon.co.uk. That's because we're passionate about bringing you the very best romantic fiction. Here are some of the advantages of shopping at www.millsandboon.co.uk:

* **Get new books first**—you'll be able to buy your favourite books one month before they hit the shops

* **Get exclusive discounts**—you'll also be able to buy our specially created monthly collections, with up to 50% off the RRP

* **Find your favourite authors**—latest news, interviews and new releases for all your favourite authors and series on our website, plus ideas for what to try next

* **Join in**—once you've bought your favourite books, don't forget to register with us to rate, review and join in the discussions

Visit **www.millsandboon.co.uk**
for all this and more today!

MILLS & BOON®

MODERN™

POWER, PASSION AND IRRESISTIBLE TEMPTATION

A sneak peek at next month's titles...

In stores from 7th April 2016:

- **Morelli's Mistress** – Anne Mather
- **Billionaire Without a Past** – Carol Marinelli
- **The Most Scandalous Ravensdale** – Melanie Milburne
- **Claiming the Royal Innocent** – Jennifer Hayward

In stores from 21st April 2016:

- **A Tycoon to Be Reckoned With** – Julia James
- **The Shock Cassano Baby** – Andie Brock
- **The Sheikh's Last Mistress** – Rachael Thomas
- **Kept at the Argentine's Command** – Lucy Ellis